Dearest Cat,
I've loved this book for
many years, and I hope you
and your boys will love it
as well.
♡ Always,
Sara

The Juniper Tree

· I ·

THE JUNIPER TREE
and Other Tales from Grimm

Selected by Lore Segal and Maurice Sendak

Translated by Lore Segal
With four tales translated by Randall Jarrell

Pictures by Maurice Sendak

· I ·

Farrar, Straus and Giroux · New York

A Note on the Translations

"Many-Fur" is translated from the text in the first edition of *Kinder- und Hausmärchen* (1812, 1815), which is more coherent than the versions in the later editions. The other tales are translated from the later texts, as reworked by the Brothers Grimm.

Randall Jarrell's translations of "The Fisherman and His Wife," "Hansel and Gretel," "The Golden Bird," and "Snow-White and the Seven Dwarfs," first published in *The Golden Bird and Other Fairy Tales of the Brothers Grimm* (Macmillan, 1962), are reprinted here.

Thanks are due to Paul Stern for saving me from mistakes in the German and for solutions in the English, at every step along the way.

L. S.

The Tales

The Pictures

VOLUME II

The Juniper Tree

· I ·

The Three Feathers

Once upon a time there was a king who had three sons; two were smart and clever but the third did not talk much, was simple, and they never called him anything but Dumbkin. When the king grew old and weak and began to think of his end, he did not know which of his sons should inherit the kingdom after him, so he said, "Go out into the world, and the one who brings home the finest carpet shall be king after my death." That there might be no quarreling, he led the three princes in front of the palace, blew three feathers into the air, and said, "As they fly, so you shall follow."

One of the feathers flew east, the other west, but the third flew straight forward, did not fly far, and dropped to the ground. Now one brother went right, the other went left, and they laughed at Dumbkin, who had to stay right there, where the third feather had fallen to the ground.

Dumbkin sat down and was sad. All of a sudden he noticed that right next to the feather was a trap door. He lifted it up and found some stairs and climbed down. He came to another door, knocked, and heard someone calling from inside:

> "Lady green and neat
> Prunefeet
> Prunefeet's puppy dog
> Prunes here and everywhere
> Quickly see who might be there."

The door opened by itself and there sat a great fat toad surrounded by a lot of little toads. The fat toad asked him what he wanted. He answered, "I would like to have the finest, most beautiful carpet," so she called over one of the young ones and said:

> "Lady green and neat
> Prunefeet
> Prunefeet's puppy dog
> Prunes here and everywhere
> Bring me that large box over there."

The young toad fetched the box and the fat toad opened it and gave Dumbkin a carpet so beautiful and fine, nothing like it could have been woven on earth. And so he thanked her and climbed back out.

The two others, however, had taken their youngest brother for a simpleton, and did not think he would ever come up with anything. "Why should we give ourselves a lot of trouble looking," they said, and each got hold of the first shepherd's wife he met, took the rough clothes off her back, and brought them to the king. At that same moment came Dumbkin with his beautiful carpet, and when the king saw it he was amazed and said, "By rights the kingdom belongs to the youngest." But the two others left their father no peace and said it was impossible for Dumbkin, who had no sense at all, to become king and begged him to set a new trial. And so the father said, "The one who brings home the most beautiful ring shall inherit the kingdom," led the three brothers outside, and blew into the air the three feathers which they were to follow. Again the two eldest went east and west but Dumbkin's feather blew straight forward and fell to the ground right next to the door in the earth. And so he climbed back down to the fat toad and told her that he needed the most beautiful ring. She had them bring her the big box right away and gave him a ring that glittered with brilliants and was so beautiful no goldsmith on earth could have made it. The two eldest laughed at Dumbkin trying to find a golden ring and took no trouble at all; each knocked out the nails from the iron ring of an old wagon wheel and brought it to the king. But when Dumbkin showed his golden ring, the father once again said, "The kingdom belongs to him." The two eldest would not give up tormenting the king until he set still a third trial and made a proclamation that he should have the kingdom who brought home the most beautiful woman. Once again he blew

the three feathers into the air and they flew as they had flown the two other times.

And so Dumbkin, without further ado, went down to the fat toad and said, "I am to bring home the most beautiful woman." "Well, well," said the toad, "the most beautiful woman, eh? That's not so easy to come by, but you shall have her all the same." She gave him a hollow carrot that was harnessed to six mice. But Dumbkin said, very sadly, "What am I to do with this?" The toad answered, "Just you set one of my little toads inside." And so he took one out of the circle at random and put her in the yellow coach, and as soon as she sat inside she turned into the most beautiful young lady, the carrot turned into a carriage, and the six mice into horses. And so he kissed her and galloped off with the horses and brought her to the king. The brothers had arrived too, but they had taken no trouble to look for a beautiful woman and each had brought home the first peasant woman he had come across. When the king saw them, he said, "The youngest shall have the kingdom after my death." But the two eldest deafened the king's ears with their clamor: "We cannot allow Dumbkin to be king!" and they demanded that the prize should go to him whose woman could jump through the ring that hung down from the middle of the hall. Surely, they thought, the peasant women will be good at something like this, they are strong enough, but the delicate young lady will jump herself to death. The old king agreed to this as well, and so the two peasant women jumped, and though they managed to get through they were so clumsy they fell and broke their coarse arms and legs. Then the beautiful lady whom Dumbkin had brought leaped through as lightly as a deer, and all opposition had to come to an end.

And thus Dumbkin received the crown and long and wisely did he reign.

Hans My Hedgehog

Once upon a time there was a peasant who had plenty of the world's goods, but rich as he might be his happiness was not complete because he had no children with his wife. Often, on the way to town, the other peasants would make fun of him and ask him why he had no children, and once he got angry and when he came home he said, "I *will* have a child, even if it's a hedgehog." And so his wife bore a child that was a hedgehog above and a boy below and when she saw the child she was horrified and said, "Now look what you've

11

done, you have put a curse on us," and the man said, "There's nothing we can do about it now. The boy must be christened, but we won't have any godfather." The woman said, "Nor can we call him anything but Hans my Hedgehog." When he was christened, the parson said, "He can't sleep in a regular bed because of his spikes." And so they made up a little straw for him behind the stove and Hans my Hedgehog was put down on it. Nor could his mother suckle him because he would have pricked her with his spikes. So there he lay behind the oven for eight years and his father got tired of him and thought, If he would only die! He did not die, however, but went on lying there. Now it so happened that there was a fair in town and the peasant wanted to go, and so he asked his wife what he should bring home for her. "A little meat, a couple of rolls, things for the house," said she. Then he asked the maid, and she wanted a pair of clogs and some embroidered stockings. Finally he asked, "Hans my Hedgehog, and what would you like?" "Daddy," said he, "why don't you bring me some bagpipes?" Now when the farmer came home, he gave his wife what he had brought for

her, meat and rolls; then he gave the maid the clogs
and the embroidered stockings, and finally he went behind the stove and gave Hans my Hedgehog the bagpipes. And when Hans my Hedgehog had his bagpipes
he said, "Daddy, why don't you go to the smithy and
have them shoe my cockerel for me, then I will ride
away and never come back any more." The father was
glad to be rid of him and the cock was shod, and when
that was done Hans my Hedgehog got up on its back
and rode off, taking with him pigs and donkeys to tend
out in the forest. In the forest he made the cock fly him
up into a tall tree and there he sat and tended the
donkeys and the pigs and sat many years until the herds
were very big, and his father didn't know anything about
him. And sitting in his tree he blew his bagpipes and
made music and the music was very beautiful. Once a
king who had lost his way came riding past and heard
the music and it puzzled him and he sent his servant
to go and look around and see where it might come
from. The servant looked all around but saw nothing
except a little animal sitting up in a tree; it looked like
a cock with a hedgehog sitting on top of it and that's

what was making the music. And so the king told the servant to go and ask him why he was sitting there and if he happened to know the way home to his kingdom. And so Hans my Hedgehog climbed down from the tree and said he would show him the way if the king would sign over and promise to give him the first thing that came to meet him when he arrived home in his palace. The king thought, I can easily do that; Hans my Hedgehog won't understand a word and I can write down anything I want. And so the king took pen and ink and wrote something down. That done, Hans my Hedgehog showed him the way and he arrived home safely. Only his daughter, seeing him from afar, was so happy she ran to meet him and kissed him and he remembered Hans my Hedgehog and told her what had happened and how he was supposed to sign over to a strange little animal the first thing that came to meet him when he arrived home and how this animal had sat astride a cock the way you sit on a horse, and had made beautiful music, but what he had written was that he should not have it, because Hans my Hedgehog couldn't even read. The princess was glad, and said it was just as well, be-

cause she never, never would have gone.

But Hans my Hedgehog tended the donkeys and pigs, kept cheerful, sat in the tree, and blew his bagpipes. Now it so happened that another king came riding by with his attendants and runners and had lost his way and did not know how to get home because the forest was so very large. He too heard the beautiful music from far away and asked his runner what it could be and told him to go and take a look. And so the runner went and stood under the tree and saw the cock with Hans my Hedgehog sitting on it. The runner asked him what he was up to up there. "I'm tending my donkeys and pigs and what can I do for you?" The runner told him that they were lost and didn't know how to get home to their kingdom and could he show them the way. And so the cock and Hans my Hedgehog came down from the tree and he promised to show the old king the way home if the king would promise him the first thing that came to meet him in the royal palace. The king said, "Yes," and made an agreement with Hans my Hedgehog in writing, promising that he should have it. That done, Hans my Hedgehog rode ahead on his cock and showed him the way and the king reached the kingdom in safety. When he came into the palace, there was great joy. Now the king had an only daughter and she was very beautiful, and she ran to meet him, threw her arms around his neck, and kissed him and was happy her old father was home again. And she asked him where in the whole wide world he had been all this time and he told her how he had lost his way and might never have come back at all, but as he was riding through a great forest, there had been someone half like a hedgehog, half like a man, sitting astride a cock in a tall tree, who made beautiful music, and he had helped him and showed him the way but in return he had promised him the first thing that came to meet him in the royal palace and that was she and now he was very sorry. But she promised him that she would gladly go with him, when he came, for her old father's sake.

But Hans my Hedgehog went on tending his pigs and his pigs got more pigs and there got to be so many that the whole forest was full of pigs. And so Hans my Hedgehog did not feel like living in the forest any longer and sent a message to his father, to have all the stables in the village cleared because he was coming with a herd so big that whoever felt like butchering could butcher. His father was sorry to hear this because he thought Hans my Hedgehog had died long ago. But Hans my Hedgehog mounted his cock, drove his pigs ahead of him into the village, and had them butchered. Well, was there ever a slaughtering and a hacking! One could hear it at a two hours' distance. Afterward Hans my Hedgehog said, "Daddy, have the cock shod for me again at the smithy, then I'm going to ride away and never come back as long as I live." And so his father had the cock shod and was glad that Hans my Hedgehog was not coming home any more.

Hans my Hedgehog rode off into the first kingdom, where the king had made a proclamation that if anyone came riding on a cock and carrying bagpipes everyone should hit and stab and shoot him to stop him from coming into the castle. Now when Hans my Hedgehog came riding up, they rushed him with their bayonets, but he set spur to his cock and flew over the gates and straight to the king's window. There he let himself down and called to the king to give him what he had promised or he would take his life and his daughter's life as well. And so the king coaxed his daughter to go to him and save his life and her own. And she dressed herself all in white and her father gave her a carriage with six horses, and splendid attendants, and great treasure. She got in and sat down beside Hans my Hedgehog with his cock and bagpipes, then they said goodbye and drove off and the king thought he would never see her again. However, it did not turn out as he had imagined, because when they got a little way out of town, Hans my Hedgehog took off her beautiful clothes and pricked her with his hedgehog skin till she was all bloody and said, "This is the reward for your treachery. Go away, I don't want you," and with that he chased her home and she was disgraced her life long.

But Hans my Hedgehog rode on, sitting astride his cock and carrying his bagpipes, to the kingdom of the second king whom he had shown the way. This king had proclaimed that if anyone like Hans my Hedgehog came along, they should present arms, shout hurray, escort him in, and bring him to the royal palace. Now when the princess saw him she was horrified because he did look so very peculiar, but she thought there was nothing to do about it because she had given her promise to her father. And so she welcomed Hans my Hedgehog and they were married and he had to sit at the royal board and she sat at his side and they ate and drank. Now in the evening when it was time to go to bed, she was frightened of his prickles but he told her not to be afraid, nothing would hurt her, and he asked the king to send four men to stand guard outside the door of the room and build a great fire, and when he went in to go to bed he would crawl out of his hedgehog skin and leave it lying in front of the bed and then the men should rush in and throw it into the fire and stay until the fire had consumed it. Now when the clock struck eleven he went into the room, stripped off his hedgehog skin, and left it lying in front of the bed and the men quickly came and fetched it and threw it into the fire, and when the fire had consumed it the curse was broken and there he lay in the bed, a human, except that he was coal-black as if he had been burned. So the king sent for his physician, who washed him with good salves and anointed him, and he became white and was a beautiful young gentleman. When the princess saw him she was glad and the next morning they rose joyfully, ate, and drank, and only now was the wedding celebrated in earnest and Hans my Hedgehog received the kingdom from the old king.

When several years had gone by, he took his wife to visit his father and told him that he was his son but the father said he didn't have a son, his only one had been born a hedgehog with spikes and had gone out into the world. Then he made himself known and the old father was happy and went home with them into his kingdom.

> And now my story's done
> And runs
> To visit little John.

The Story of One
Who Set Out to Study Fear

A father had two sons of whom the eldest was sensible and clever and good at everything but the youngest was stupid and could not understand or learn anything. People would look at him and say, "That one is going to give his father nothing but trouble." Now when there was anything to be done, it was the eldest who always had to do it, but if the father wanted something brought and it was already late, perhaps even nighttime, and the way led through the churchyard or some other eerie place, he would say, "Oh, Father, no! I'm not going, it

makes my flesh creep!" because he was afraid. Or, evenings, in front of the fire, when they told stories that
make shivers run down your spine, the listeners would
say, "Doesn't that make your flesh creep?" The youngest sat in his corner and listened too and could never
understand what they meant. "They're always saying,
'It makes my flesh creep! It makes my flesh creep!' It
doesn't make *my* flesh creep. This must be another skill
I don't understand anything about."

Now one day it happened that the father said to him,
"Listen, you over there in the corner! You're growing big
and strong and you too will have to learn something with
which to earn a living. Look at your brother, he always
tries to do his best, but as for you! It's a waste of breath
even talking to you!" "Oh, but, Father," answered the
boy, "there is something I would really like to learn.
What I would like to learn, if possible, is how to make
my flesh creep. That's something I don't understand
anything about yet." The eldest son laughed when he
heard this, and thought, "Good Lord, what a fathead my
brother is! He'll never amount to anything as long as he
lives. What would become a hook must crook itself be-

24

times." The father sighed and answered, "Your flesh will creep soon enough, but that'll never earn you a living."

Soon after this, the sexton came to call and the father told him about the trouble he was having with his youngest son, how useless he was, that he knew nothing and was going to learn nothing. "Just think, when I asked him how he was going to earn his living, he wanted, of all things, to learn how to make his flesh creep!" "If that's all he wants," answered the sexton, "there's something he can learn at my house. Let him come and live with me, I'll soon shape him up." The father was content, because he thought: At least it will take some of the rough edges off the boy. And so the sexton took the boy into his house and his job was to ring the bell. After a few days, the sexton woke him around midnight and told him to get up, climb into the church tower, and toll the bell. You're going to learn what it's like when your flesh creeps, he thought, and secretly went ahead; when the boy came up and turned around to take hold of the bell rope, there, standing on the stair opposite the louvers, he saw a white shape. "Who goes there?" he called, but the shape gave no answer, stood and never stirred. "Answer me," called the boy, "or get out! You've got no business here at night." But the sexton kept standing there, motionless, to make the boy think it was a ghost. And for the second time the boy called, "What are you doing here? Speak up, if you're a true man, or I'll throw you down the stairs." The sexton thought, "He doesn't really mean it," didn't make a sound, and stood as if he were made of stone. So the boy called out for the third time and when that did no good he took a run and pushed the ghost down the stairs, so that it fell ten steps and remained lying in a corner. Thereupon he tolled the bell and went home, lay down in his bed without a word, and went back to sleep. The sexton's wife waited for her husband a long time but he didn't and didn't come back. In the end she got worried, woke the boy up, and asked, "You don't know what happened to my husband, do you? He climbed into the tower ahead of you." "No," answered the boy, "but there was somebody standing on the stair opposite the louvers and when he didn't answer me and wouldn't go away either, I took him for some rascal and pushed him downstairs. Why don't you go over and

then you'll see if it was your husband, and if it was I'm
very sorry." Off ran the woman and found her husband
lying in a corner, whimpering, and he had a broken leg.

She carried him down and then she ran to the boy's
father screaming and hollering. "Your boy," she cried,
"has caused a great tragedy. He threw my husband
down the stairs, so that he broke a leg. Get this good-
for-nothing out of our house." The father was horror-
stricken and came running and scolded the boy. "What
kind of wicked trick is this! The devil himself must have
put you up to it." "But, Father," answered he, "just listen to me, will you! I didn't do anything wrong. There
he stood in the night, and looked like he was up to no
good. I didn't know who it was and I warned him three
times to speak up or go away." "Ah," said the father,
"with you I will have nothing but grief. Go on! Get out
of my sight, I don't want to look at you any more." "Oh,
all right, Father, that's fine by me, just wait till daylight,
and then I'll go away and learn to make my flesh creep,
so that at least I'll have some skill with which to earn
my living." "Learn what you want," said the father, "it's
all the same to me. Here are fifty thalers, take them and

go out into the wide world and don't tell anybody where you come from or who your father is, because I am ashamed of you." "Right you are, Father. Whatever you say. If that's what you want, I can do that."

Now at daybreak the boy put his fifty thalers in his pocket and walked out onto the great highway, mumbling to himself, "If I could only make my flesh creep! Oh, if my flesh would only creep!" A man walking along behind him heard this conversation the boy was having with himself and when they had walked awhile, and come within sight of the gallows, the man said, "Look, there's the tree on which seven have had their wedding with the ropemaker's daughter and are learning how to fly. Go sit underneath, wait till night comes and it will make your flesh creep all right." "If that's all there is to it," answered the boy, "it's easy. If my flesh really learns to creep as fast as that, you can have my fifty thalers. Come back and see me in the morning." So the boy walked over to the gallows, sat down underneath, and waited till evening, and because he was cold, he made a fire. But around midnight the wind blew so bitterly he could not keep warm, and as the wind set the hanged men moving to and fro and knocked one against the other, he thought: You're freezing down here by your fire, no wonder they are freezing and fidgeting up there. And because he had a kind heart, he got the ladder, climbed up, untied one after the other, and brought all seven of them down. Then he stoked the fire, blew on it, and set them around it so they might warm themselves. But they sat and didn't stir, and the fire caught their clothes, so he said, "Take care, or I'll string you up again." But the dead men didn't hear, said nothing, and let their rags go on burning, and so he became annoyed and said, "If you won't take care of yourselves, I can't help you. I don't want to burn to a cinder along with you," and strung them up again, one after the other. Now he sat down by his fire and went to sleep and next morning the man came and wanted his fifty thalers and said, "Now do you know what it's like to feel your flesh creep?" "No," answered he. "How am I supposed to know? Those characters up there never opened their mouths and were so stupid they let the few old rags they have on their bodies catch fire." So the man saw he wasn't going to collect any fifty thalers that day, and went away saying, "I never met one like that before."

The boy too went on his way and started talking to himself again. "Oh, if I could only make my flesh creep! Oh, if my flesh would only creep!" A wagoner who was striding along behind him heard and asked, "Who are you?" "I don't know," answered the boy. The wagoner went on questioning him: "Where are you from?" "I don't know." "Who is your father?" "I mustn't tell." "What's that you keep muttering between your teeth?" "Oh," answered the boy, "I want my flesh to creep, but no one can teach me how." "Stop babbling," said the wagoner. "Come with me and I'll see if I can't find you a place with a good master somewhere." So the boy went along with the wagoner and in the evening they came to an inn where they could spend the night, and as they entered the room the boy began again very loudly: "If I could only make my flesh creep. If my flesh would only creep." The innkeeper heard him, laughed, and said, "If that's what you need to make you happy, there's a great opportunity for you right here." "Oh, be quiet," said the innkeeper's wife. "There's a lot of smart alecks have already paid with their lives and wouldn't it be a shame

if these pretty eyes never saw the light of day again."
But the boy said, "Let it be ever so hard, I want to learn
it once and for all. That's what I set out to study." He
left the innkeeper no peace until he told him that not
far away there stood an enchanted castle where a man
could certainly learn what it's like when your flesh
creeps by just going up and watching for three nights,
and that the king had promised his daughter's hand to
anyone who dared, and she was the most beautiful girl
under the sun; and that there was a great treasure in
the castle, guarded by evil spirits, and then it would be
freed and there was enough to make any poor man rich.
Many's the one who had gone in, but no one had come
out again. And so the next morning the boy went to the
king and said, "If you please, I would like to watch in
the enchanted castle for three nights." The king looked
at the boy and because he liked him he said, "You may
ask for any three things, so long as they're not live, to
take into the castle with you." And so the boy answered,
"Well, then I want fire, and a lathe, and a bench with a
vise and the whittling knife that goes with it."

The king had everything carried into the castle while

33

it was still daylight, and when night was drawing in, the boy went up, made himself a bright fire in one of the rooms, put up the bench with the knife beside it, and sat down on the lathe. "If I could only make my flesh creep," he said, "but I'm never going to learn it here!" Toward midnight he went to stoke his fire and as he was blowing on it there suddenly came a screeching out of the corners. "Ow, miaow, how cold we are!" "You fools," he called out, "what are you screaming about? If you're cold, come and sit by the fire and warm yourselves." No sooner had he spoken than two big black cats came out with a mighty leap, sat down on either side, and looked at him ferociously with their fiery eyes. After a while, when they had warmed themselves, they said, "Friend, how about a little hand of cards?" "Why not?" answered he. "But first show me your paws." And so they stretched out their claws. "My," said he, "don't you have long nails! Wait, first I've got to trim them for you." And so he took them by the scruff of the neck, lifted them onto his bench, and screwed their paws fast. "One look at your fingers," said he, "and I've lost my yen for any hand of cards with you," and then he killed them and threw them into the water outside. No sooner had he made an end of those two and was about to sit down by his fire than out of every nook and cranny there came black cats and black dogs on smoldering chains, always more and more, until there was not one safe spot for him to stand. They screamed abominably, climbed all over his fire, tore it up, and tried to put it out. For a while he watched quietly, but then it got too much for him, and he took his whittling knife and cried, "Away with you, scum!" and started to hit at them. Some ran away, the others he killed and threw out into the pond, and when he came back, he blew a fresh fire from the embers and warmed himself. And as he sat there, his eyes would not stay open and he felt like going to sleep, and so he looked around and saw a big bed in a corner. "Just what I need," said he, and went and lay down in it, but just as he was going to close his eyes, the bed began to ride away of its own accord and rode all over the whole castle. "That's all right by me," he said. "But can't you go a bit faster, please." The bed rolled along as if it had six horses in harness, over the threshold, upstairs and

35

down. All of a sudden, crash bang, it turned over and lay upside down on top of him like a mountain, but he tossed covers and pillows into the air, climbed out, and said, "Now let someone else take a ride," and lay down by his fire and slept till daybreak. In the morning the king came, and when he saw him lying there on the ground, he thought the spirits had taken his life and that he was dead, and so he said, "What a pity for this beautiful young man." The boy heard him, sat up, and said, "It hasn't come to that yet," and the king was amazed but very pleased and asked him how he had got on. "Pretty well," answered he. "One night has passed and so will the two others." When he came back to the inn, the innkeeper stared at him wide-eyed. "I didn't think," said he, "that I'd ever see you alive again. Now have you learned what it's like to have your flesh creep?" "No," he said. "There's no help for me. If only someone could explain it to me."

The second night he went back into the old castle, sat down by the fire, and started up his old song: "If my flesh would only creep!" As midnight approached, one could hear a rumbling and a clattering, first softly, then stronger and stronger. Then it was quiet for a bit. At last, with a loud screech, half of a man came down the chimney and fell right in front of him. "Hey there!" cried he, "there's a half missing. This is not enough." And so the din started all over again: there was a heaving and a howling and out fell the other half as well. "Wait," said he, "first let me make up the fire a little for you." When he had done so, he looked around again and the two halves had joined together and there, in his place on the lathe, sat a grisly man. "That was not part of the bargain," said the boy. "That's my seat." The man tried to shove him away but the boy would not give in and pushed him off by main force and sat down again in his own place. And so then still more men kept falling out, one after the other, and they brought nine dead men's bones and two skulls, set up a game of ninepins, and began to play. The boy felt like playing too, and said, "Listen, can I play?" "Yes, if you have money." "Plenty of money," answered he, "but your bowls are not quite round." And so he took the skulls, put them in his lathe, and turned them until they were round. "There. Now they'll roll better," he

said. "Hey, this is fun!" He played with them and lost
a little money, but when midnight tolled, everything
disappeared in front of his eyes. He lay down and went
quietly to sleep. The next morning came the king to
inquire after him. "How did it go this time?" he asked.
"I played at ninepins," answered he, "and lost a couple
of pennies." "And it didn't make your flesh creep?"
"Heavens no," said he, "I had a good time. Oh, if I only
knew what it feels like to have one's flesh creep!"

On the third night he sat down again on his lathe
and said crossly, "If my flesh would only *creep*." When
it was quite late, six tall men came carrying a coffin.
The boy said, "Aha! That must be my cousin who
died a couple of days ago," beckoned with his finger and
cried, "Come in, cousin, come along in." They set the
coffin down on the floor and he went over and took the
lid off. There was a dead man lying inside. He touched
his face and it was cold as ice. "Wait," said he, "I'll warm
you up a little," went to the fire, warmed his hand, and
laid it against the dead man's face, but he remained cold,
and so he took him out, sat down in front of the fire, and
laid him on his lap and rubbed his arms to set the blood

in motion. When that did no good either, it came to him that when two lie in bed together they warm each other up, so he put him in the bed, lay down beside him, and pulled up the covers. And after a little while the dead man did warm up and began to stir, and the boy said, "There, you see, cousin? I warmed you up, didn't I?" But the dead man lifted his voice and cried, "Now I will strangle you!" "What," said he, "is this the thanks I get? You're going right back in your coffin," picked him up, threw him in, and closed the lid; then the six men came and carried him away. "My flesh will not and will not creep," said he, "I'll never learn it here as long as I live."

Then there entered a man who was bigger than all the rest, and looked horrible and old, with a long white beard. "Wretch!" cried he. "Now you shall learn how it feels to have your flesh creep: you are going to die." "Not so fast," answered the boy. "If I'm the one to do the dying, I have to be there, don't I?" "I'll catch you yet," said the monster. "Take it easy, now," said the boy. "You talk big, but I'm as strong as you are and probably stronger." "That remains to be seen," said the old man. "If you are stronger, I will let you go. Come, we'll put it to the test." And so he led him along dark passages to a blacksmith's forge, took an ax, and with one blow drove the anvil into the ground. "I can do better than that," said the boy, and walked over to the other anvil. The old man came and stood next to him to watch, and his white beard hung down. And so the boy took hold of the ax and with one blow split the anvil in two and caught the old man's beard in the middle. "Now I've got you," said the boy, "and it's you who's going to die." And he picked up an iron bar and began to beat the old man until he whimpered and begged him to stop and promised to give him great riches. The boy pulled out the ax and let him go. The old man led him back to the castle and showed him a cellar with three chests full of gold. "Of these," said he, "one part is for the poor, another belongs to the king, the third is yours." With that, midnight struck, the spirit disappeared, and there stood the boy in the dark. "I'll get myself out of here," said he, groped around, found the way into the room with the fire, and fell asleep. The next morning came the king and said, "Now you must have learned what it is to have your flesh creep." "No," said he. "Whatever can it be? My dead cousin was here, and a man with a beard came and showed me a lot of money, but nobody said a word about creeping flesh." The king said, "You have set the castle free and shall marry my daughter." "That's all very well," answered he, "but I still don't know a thing about getting my flesh to creep."

And so the gold was brought up and the wedding celebrated, but the young king, dearly though he loved his wife, and happy though he was, still kept saying, "If I could only make my flesh creep, oh, if my flesh would only creep," until the queen got angry. Her maid said, "I know what to do. His flesh is going to learn all about creeping." She went out to the brook that flowed through the garden and had them bring her a bucket full of minnows. At night, when the young king was asleep, his wife had to pull off the covers and pour the bucketful of cold water and the minnows on him. The little fish squirmed all over him, and he woke up and cried, "Something is making my flesh creep! Dear wife, how my flesh is creeping! Ah, now I know what it's like when one's flesh creeps."

41

Brother and Sister

Brother took his little sister by the hand and said, "Since our mother died we have not had one happy hour. Stepmother beats us every day and when we want to come to her she kicks us away with her foot. The hard crusts of leftover bread, that's what we get to eat; the little dog under the table has it better—she sometimes throws him a tidbit. Merciful God, if our mother knew! Come, we will go out into the wide world together." All day they walked over meadows, fields, and stony paths and when it rained sister said, "God and our hearts are weeping together." In the evening they came into a great forest and were so tired from misery, hunger, and the long journey that they sat down in a hollow tree and went to sleep.

When they awoke next morning, the sun already shone high in the heavens and it was hot inside the tree, and so brother said, "I'm thirsty. If I knew where to find a spring, I would go and drink. I think I hear one murmuring." Brother got up and took sister by the hand and they went to look for the spring. The wicked stepmother, however, was a witch and had seen the children go off together and she had sneaked after them, secretly, the way witches sneak, and put a spell on every spring in the forest. Now when they found a spring leaping and glittering over the stones and brother wanted to drink, sister heard it murmuring and it was saying, "Whoever drinks me, whoever drinks me, will be a tiger, will be a tiger." And so sister cried, "Dear brother, please don't drink or you will become a wild beast and tear me to pieces." Brother did not drink, although he was so very thirsty, and said, "I will wait for the next spring." When they came to the second spring, sister heard how this one too spoke, "Whoever drinks me, whoever drinks me, will be a wolf, will be a wolf," and so she cried, "Dear brother, please don't drink or you will become a wolf and devour me." Brother did not drink and said, "I will wait till we come to the next spring, but then I must drink whatever you may say, I am so very, very thirsty." And when they came to the third spring, sister heard it murmuring and how it was saying, "Whoever drinks me, whoever drinks me, will be a deer, will be a deer." Sister said, "Please, brother, do not drink, or you will become a deer and run away from me," but brother had already knelt down beside the spring and bent his head and when the first drops touched his lips he lay there as a young fawn.

Now the sister wept over the poor bewitched little brother and the little fawn wept too and sat sorrowfully beside her. And so in the end the girl said, "Don't worry, my little fawn, because I will never, never leave you." Then she untied her golden garter and put it around the neck of the little deer and picked reeds and braided them into a soft rope which she fastened to the little animal and led it farther and ever deeper into the forest. And when they had gone a long, long way, they came to a hut and the girl looked in and saw that it was empty and she thought, Here we can stay and spend our lives. And so she collected leaves and moss to make a soft bed for the deer, and every morning she went out and found roots and berries and nuts for herself, and for the deer she brought tender grasses which it ate out of her hand and it was happy and gamboled all around her. At night, when sister was tired and had said her prayers, she laid her head on the fawn's back and that was her pillow on which she fell gently asleep. And if only brother had his human form, it would have been a lovely life.

And so it went for a while, that they were all alone in the wilderness. It happened that the king of the land brought a great hunting party to the forest. The blowing of the horn, the barking of the dogs, the cheerful hallooing of the huntsmen rang through the trees and the deer heard it and longed so to be part of it all. "Ah," it said to sister, "let me go out and join the hunt. I cannot bear it any longer," and begged and begged until she had to give in. "But," said she to the deer, "mind you come home by nightfall. I will lock my door against these wild huntsmen, and so I shall know it's you, knock and say, 'My sister, let me in,' and if you don't say these words, I won't unlock my door!" Now the deer leaped out the door and away and felt oh, so wonderfully happy in the free and open air. The king and his huntsmen saw the beautiful animal and gave chase but they could not catch up with it. Every time they thought they had it, it leaped the bushes and disappeared. When it grew dark, the deer ran to the hut, knocked, and said, "My sister, let me in," and the little door opened and it came in and rested all night on its soft bed. Next morning the hunt began anew and when the deer heard the hunting horn and the Oho! of the huntsmen, it had no peace and said, "Sister, open the door, I must be out there too." Sister opened the door for the deer and said, "But tonight come back and say the words I taught you." When the king and his huntsmen saw the little deer with its gold collar, they gave chase, but it was too fast and nimble for them. And so it went all that day and by evening

the huntsmen had the deer surrounded and one wounded it a little in the foot so that it limped slowly away. One of the huntsmen stole after it till it came to a hut and he heard how it called out, "My sister, let me in," and saw the door open and close behind it. The huntsman took in everything and went to the king and told him what he had seen and heard, and the king said, "Tomorrow we hunt again."

But the sister was very much frightened when she saw her little fawn had been wounded. She washed away the blood, laid herbs on the wound, and said, "Go to your bed, little deer, so you will get well." But the wound was so slight, by next morning the deer no longer felt anything, and when it again heard the excitement of the hunt, it said, "I cannot bear it, I must be out there too. I won't be so easy to catch." Sister wept and said, "Now they will kill you and I'll be all alone in the forest and the whole world has forsaken me. I will not let you go." "Then I must die of grief here," answered the fawn. "When I hear the hunting horn I feel myself jumping out of my boots." And so there was nothing for it; sister unlocked the door with a heavy heart and the deer leaped away into the forest healthy and so happy. When the king caught sight of it, he said to his huntsmen, "Now give chase until nighttime, but don't any of you do it harm." As soon as the sun had set, the king said to the huntsman, "Now come and show me the hut in the woods," and when he stood in front of the door he knocked and called, "Dear sister, let me in," and the door opened and the king stepped inside and there stood a girl more beautiful than any he had ever seen. The girl was frightened when she saw that it was not her little deer who came in but a man wearing a golden crown on his head. But the king looked at her so kindly and gave her his hand and said, "Will you come to my palace with me and be my dear wife?"

"Oh, yes," answered the girl, "but the fawn must come too because I could never, never leave it."

Said the king, "It shall stay with you as long as you live and shall want for nothing." At this moment it came leaping in and so the sister put it on the leash of rushes and held the leash in her own hand and led the deer away with her out of the hut in the woods.

The king took the lovely girl on his horse and brought her to his palace, where the wedding was celebrated with great splendor, and so now she was queen and for a long while they lived happily together; the deer was well beloved and well tended and gamboled all over the palace grounds. Meanwhile, the wicked stepmother who had caused the children to go out into the world was sure that sister had been torn to pieces by wild animals in the forest and that the fawn had been shot dead by the huntsmen. Now, when she heard how happy and prosperous they were, envy and malice stirred in her heart and left her no peace and she could think of nothing but how she might bring calamity upon them both. Her real daughter, who was ugly as sin and had only one eye, heaped reproaches on her and said, "To become queen is a happiness that should be mine by rights."

"Just you wait," the old woman said to comfort her, "when the time comes, I will be ready."

Now the queen brought a lovely little boy into the world, but the king happened to be away hunting. The old witch took on the guise of the waiting woman, stepped into the room where the queen lay, and told the sick woman, "Come, your bath is ready. It will do you good and give you new strength. Quick, before it gets cold." Her daughter was at hand and they carried the queen, who was still weak, into the bathhouse, laid her in the bath, closed the door, and ran away. But they had made up a fire in the bathhouse that was as hot as the fires of hell, so that the beautiful young queen soon stifled to death.

After that the old woman took her daughter, put a cap on her head, and laid her in bed in the queen's place. She even gave her the form and features of the queen, but the lost eye she could not give her back. So the king would not notice, she made her lie on the side where she had no eye. In the evening, when the king came home and heard that a little son had been born to him, he was overjoyed and went to his dear wife's bedside to see how she was, but the old woman quickly cried, "For God's sake, leave the curtains drawn. The queen must not look into the light yet and must stay quiet." The king stepped back and did not know that a wrong queen lay in the bed.

But at midnight, when everybody was asleep, the old nurse who sat beside the cradle, and was the only person still awake, saw how the door opened and the true queen came in. She lifted the child out of the cradle, took it on her arm, and nursed it. Then she plumped the pillow, laid the child down, and covered it with the quilt. Nor did she forget the little deer, went into the corner where it lay and stroked its back, and went silently out of the door. Next morning the nurse asked the watchmen if anyone had come into the palace that night, but they answered, "No, we saw nobody." And so she came many a night and spoke never a word. The nurse always saw her but did not dare tell anyone about it.

Now when some time had passed, the queen began to speak in the night, saying, "How is my child? How is my fawn? Now I come twice more, and never again."

The nurse did not answer her but, when she had disappeared again, went to the king and told him everything. Said the king, "Dear God, what is this! Tomorrow night I will watch by the child." In the evening he went into the nursery and at midnight the queen appeared again and said, "How is my child? How is my fawn? Now I come once more and never again," and cared for the child as always, before she disappeared. The king did not dare speak to her but the next night he watched again and again she spoke: "How is my child? How is my fawn? Now I am here and never again." And the king could not contain himself, rushed to her, and said, "You are none other than my dear wife." And she answered, "Yes, I am your dear wife," and that moment, by the grace of God, she received her life again and was fresh and rosy and well. Then she told the king what the wicked witch and her daughter had done. The king had them both brought to the court and judgment was pronounced upon them. The daughter was taken into the forest where the wild beasts tore her to pieces, but the witch was put in the fire and miserably burned to death. When she had turned to ashes, the little fawn changed back to its human form, and brother and sister lived happily together to the end of their lives.

Spindle, Shuttle, and Needle

Once upon a time there was a girl who lost her father and mother when she was still a little child. At the far end of the village, all alone in her cottage, lived her godmother, who supported herself by spinning, weaving, and sewing. The old woman took the orphan in, encouraged her to work hard, and brought her up in the fear of the Lord.

When the girl was fifteen years old, the godmother became ill and called the child to her bed and said, "Dear daughter, I feel my end drawing near. I leave you this house so you will be protected from wind and weather, and spindle, shuttle, and needle, so you can earn your keep." Then she laid her hands on the child's head, blessed her, and said, "Keep God in your heart, and all will be well with you." Then she closed her eyes, and when they carried her away to lay her in the earth, the girl walked behind the coffin, weeping bitterly, and paid her the last respects.

Now the girl lived all alone in the cottage and worked hard, spun, wove, and sewed, and the blessing of that good old woman lay on everything she did. It was as if flax increased of itself in that room, and when she had woven a piece of cloth or a carpet, or sewed a shirt, it always found a buyer who would pay her handsomely, so that she was never in need, and even had something over to share with others.

About this time the son of the king was traveling around the country looking for a bride. He could not choose a poor girl and did not want a rich one, so he said, "I will marry the girl who is at once the poorest and the richest." When he came to the village where the girl lived, he asked, as always, who was the richest in the place and who was the poorest. They named the richest first; the poorest, they said, was the girl who lived in the cottage at the far end of the village. The richest girl was sitting in front of her door, all decked out, and when she saw the prince coming she rose, walked up to him, and curtsied. He looked at her, said never a word, and rode on. When he came to the house of the poor one, the girl was not at the door but sat inside her little room. He drew rein and looked in at the window, through which the bright sun shone, and saw the girl sitting at her spindle, busily spinning. She looked up, and when she saw the prince looking in, she blushed from head to toe, lowered her eyes, and went on spinning; whether the thread came out as evenly as usual I don't know, but she spun and spun until the prince had ridden on his way. Then she walked to the window and opened it, saying, "How hot it is in this room," but she kept looking after him as long as she could make out the white feather on his hat.

Inside her room she sat down again to her work and went on spinning, and a little verse which the old woman used to say, sometimes, when she was working came into the girl's mind, and so she sat and she sang:

> "Spindle, spindle, one two three,
> Bring my suitor home to me."

And guess what happened! The spindle leaped from her hand and out the door and when, in her surprise, she got up to look after it, she saw it dancing gaily away over the fields, drawing a shining golden thread behind it, until it was out of sight. As the girl did not have another spindle, she took up the shuttle, sat down at her loom, and began to weave. But the spindle danced on and just as the thread was about to run out it caught up with the prince. "What's this?" cried he. "I think the spindle wants to show me the way." And he turned his horse and followed the golden thread back.

Meanwhile, the girl sat at her work and sang:

> "Shuttle, shuttle, three and four,
> Bring my suitor to my door."

At once the shuttle leaped from her hand and out the door, and at the threshold it began to weave a car-

pet more beautiful than anything that you have ever seen: roses and lilies bloomed along the sides, and in the middle, on a field of gold, hares and rabbits leaped through green climbing vines from which stags and does raised up their heads; among the twigs sat colorful birds that did everything but sing. The shuttle scurried here and there; it was as if everything grew of itself.

Because the shuttle had run away, the girl sat down at her sewing and held the needle in her hand and sang:

> "Needle, needle, sharp and slim,
> Dust and sweep the house for him."

And the needle leaped out of her fingers and flew to and fro in the room, quick as lightning. It was just as if invisible spirits were at work, and soon green cloth covered tables and benches, velvet the chairs; silk curtains hung down the walls. The needle had no sooner done the last stitch than through the window the girl saw the white feather on the hat of the prince, whom the spindle had brought home at the end of its golden thread. The prince dismounted, stepped over the carpet into the house, and when he came into the room there stood the girl in her wretched dress and glowed like a rose on the bush. "You are the poorest and also the richest," he said to her. "Come with me and be my bride." She was silent but she gave him her hand. And so he gave her a kiss, and led her outside, lifted her onto his horse, and brought her to the royal palace, where the wedding was celebrated in great joy. Spindle, shuttle, and needle were guarded in the treasury and paid every honor.

The Twelve Huntsmen

Once upon a time there was a prince who had a bride and he loved her very much. Now one day he was sitting beside her, feeling happy, when there came news that his father was dying and asking to see him. And so he spoke to his beloved and said, "I must go away now and leave you here but I will give you this ring as a keepsake. When I am king I will come back and fetch you home." And so he rode away. When he arrived, his father was sick to death and failing and said to him: "Dearest son, I wanted to see you once more before I die. Promise me that you will marry according to my wishes," and he named a certain princess who should be his wife. The son was so unhappy he did not stop to think and said, "Yes, dear Father, I will do whatever you wish," and so the king closed his eyes and died.

Now when the son had been proclaimed king and the period of mourning was over, he had to keep the promise he made his father, and sent to ask the princess for her hand in marriage and she was betrothed to him. When the first bride heard this she was so grieved at his faithlessness that she began to waste away. Her father said to her, "Dearest child, why are you so unhappy? Tell me what you want and it shall be yours." She considered a moment, then she said, "Dear Father, I want eleven girls exactly like me in face, figure, and stature." Said the king, "If it is possible, your wish shall be fulfilled." And so he had a search made throughout the whole realm until there were found eleven young girls who exactly resembled his daughter in face, figure, and stature.

When they came to the princess, she had twelve

hunting costumes made, one just like the other, and the eleven girls had to put on the eleven hunting costumes and she herself put on the twelfth. Then she said goodbye to her father and rode with them to the court of her former bridegroom, whom she loved so dearly. She asked him if he needed any huntsmen and if he would not take all twelve of them into his service. The king looked at her and did not know her; because they were such handsome folk he said yes, he would be glad to have them, and so they were the king's twelve huntsmen.

But the king had a lion who was a remarkable animal, because he knew everything that was hidden and secret. One evening he happened to be talking to the king and said, "You think you've got twelve huntsmen there, don't you?" "Yes," said the king. "Twelve huntsmen is what they are." Said the lion, "You're wrong. They are twelve girls." The king answered, "That's not true. How can you prove it?" "Well, why don't you have some peas strewn in your antechamber," answered the lion, "and you will see right away. Men have a firm tread; when they walk on peas not a single one so much as stirs, but girls go slipping and skipping and scuffing along so that the peas roll all around." The king liked this plan very much and had peas strewn.

But there was a servant of the king's who was fond of the huntsmen and when he heard that they were being put to the test he went and told them everything and said, "The lion wants to make the king believe that you are girls." And so the princess thanked him and spoke to her girls and said, "Force yourselves to step on the peas with a firm tread." Now the next morning, when the king had his twelve huntsmen summoned and they came into the antechamber where the peas lay, they stepped on them so firmly, with such a sure, strong tread, that not a single pea so much as stirred. And so they went away again, and the king said to the lion, "You lied to me. They walk like men." The lion answered, "They knew they were being tested and forced themselves. Why don't you have twelve spinning wheels brought in the antechamber and they will walk over and they'll take pleasure in them; men don't do that." The king liked the plan and had spinning wheels set up in the antechamber.

But the servant who had the welfare of the huntsmen at heart went and disclosed the plan to them, and when the princess was alone with her eleven girls, she said, "You must force yourselves not to turn and look at the spinning wheels." Now the next morning, when the king summoned his twelve huntsmen, they walked through the anteroom without so much as looking at the spinning wheels. And once again the king said to the lion: "You lied to me. They are men because they did not look at the spinning wheels." The lion answered, "They knew that they were being tested and they forced themselves." But the king would no longer believe the lion.

The twelve huntsmen accompanied the king on every hunt and the longer he knew them the better he loved them. Now it happened once while they were hunting that news came of the king's bride approaching. When the true bride heard this, it pained her heart so that it almost broke and she fell to the earth in a faint. The king thought something had happened to his dear huntsman, came running and wanted to help him, and drew off his glove and saw the ring he had given his first bride, and when he looked into her face he recognized her and his heart was so moved he kissed her, and when she opened her eyes he said, "You are mine and I am yours. No man on earth can change that." As for the other bride, he sent a messenger to ask her to please go back home to her kingdom because he already had a wife. He who finds his old key again does not need the new one. And so the wedding was celebrated and the lion returned to favor. Hadn't he been telling the truth all along?

Fitcher's Feathered Bird

Once upon a time there was a sorcerer and he disguised himself as a pauper, went begging from house to house, and caught the pretty girls. Nobody knew where he took them because none ever came back. One day he appeared at the door of a man who had three beautiful daughters. He looked like a poor, sick beggar and carried a basket on his back as if for the alms he was collecting. He asked for a bite of food and when the eldest girl came out to give him a piece of bread he just touched her and she could not help jumping into his basket. Then he hurried off with his powerful stride and carried her to his house, in the middle of a dark forest. Inside, everything was splendid; he gave her whatever she could wish and said, "Sweetheart, you will be happy here with me; you have everything your heart desires." So it went a couple of days and then he said, "I must go away on a journey and leave you alone for a while; here are the keys of the house, you may go anywhere and look at everything, but there is one room, which is opened with this little key here, that I forbid you under penalty of death." He also gave her an egg and said, "Look after this egg very carefully; you had better carry it wherever you go, because if it gets lost, something terrible would happen." She took the keys and the egg and promised to take good care of everything. When he had gone, she went over the house from top to bottom and looked at everything. The rooms glittered with silver and gold and it seemed to her that she had never seen such great splendor. Finally she came to the forbidden door; she meant to walk past but curiosity left her no peace. She looked at the key; it looked like any ordinary key. She put it in the keyhole and she just turned it a very little but the door sprang open. And what did she see? In the middle of the room there was a great bloody basin full of dead people hacked into pieces, and next to it stood a butcher's block with a gleaming ax on it. She was so horrified that the egg, which she had in her hand, tumbled in. She quickly picked it out and wiped off the blood, but in vain. The next moment the blood reappeared. She wiped and she scraped but she could not get it off.

It was not long before the man came back from his journey and the first thing he demanded was the key and the egg. She gave it to him but she was trembling, and he could tell from the red spots that she had been in the blood chamber. "Against my will you went in," said he, "and shall go back against yours. Your life is finished." He threw her down, dragged her in by the hair, cut her head off on the block, and hacked her to pieces so that the blood flowed all over the floor, and threw her into the basin with the rest.

"Now I'll go and get the second one," said the sorcerer, and he went back to the house disguised as a pauper begging for alms. And the second girl brought

him a piece of bread and he caught her as he had the
first by just touching her and carried her away. She
did no better than her sister, let curiosity lead her astray,
opened the blood chamber and looked inside, and on his
return paid with her life. Now he went and fetched the
third girl, but she was clever and cunning. When he had
given her the key and the egg and had gone on his
journey, she first carefully put the egg away, then she
looked all around the house and finally went into the
forbidden room. Ah, what did she see! There in the
basin lay her two dear sisters, miserably murdered and
hacked into pieces. But she set to work and gathered all
the parts and laid them in the right order, head, body,
arms, and legs. And when there was nothing missing, the
limbs began to stir and joined together and the two girls
opened their eyes and were alive again, and were happy
and kissed and hugged one another. On his arrival the
man immediately demanded key and egg, and as he
could discover no trace of blood he said, "You have
stood the test and shall be my bride." His power over
her was gone and he had to do whatever she wanted.
"Very well," she answered, "but first you must take a

basket full of gold to my father and mother, and you must carry it on your own back. Meanwhile I will get everything ready for the wedding." Then she ran to her sisters, whom she had hidden in a little back room, and said, "The moment has come when I can save you. The miscreant himself shall carry you home. But as soon as you arrive, send me help." She put both of them into the basket and covered them with gold so that one could not even see them. Then she called the sorcerer and said, "Now pick up the basket, and don't stop to rest on the way. I'll be looking out of my little window, watching you."

The sorcerer lifted the basket onto his shoulders and walked off with it. But the weight pressed so painfully into his back that the sweat ran down his face. And so he sat down to rest awhile, but right away one of the girls in the basket cried, "I'm looking through my window and can see you resting! Up you get and off you go!" He thought it was his bride calling to him and got up and went on his way. Again he wanted to sit down, but right away the voice cried, "I'm looking out of my window and see you resting! Up you get and off you go!" As often as he stopped came the voice calling him and he had to keep going until finally, groaning and out of breath, he brought the basket with the gold and the two girls into their parents' house.

At home, meanwhile, the bride was getting everything ready for the wedding and sending out the invitations to the sorcerer's friends. Then she took a skull with grinning teeth, crowned it with jewels and a garland of flowers, carried it to the attic, and let it look out of the window. When everything was ready she crawled into a barrel of honey, then she cut open the featherbed and rolled in it until she looked like some weird bird and nobody would have known her. And so she left the house and on her way she met some of the wedding guests and they asked:

"You Fitcher's feathered bird, where are you from?"
"From feathered Fitze Fitcher's house I come."
"And the young bride, what does she do?"
"From top to bottom sweeps the house like new,
  And through the attic window she is watching you."

Finally she met the bridegroom, who came wandering back slowly; he asked like the others:

"You Fitcher's feathered bird, where are you from?"
"From feathered Fitze Fitcher's house I come."
"And the young bride, what does she do?"
"From top to bottom sweeps the house like new,
  And through the attic window she is watching you."

The bridegroom looked up and saw the skull all decked out and thought it was his bride and nodded to her and waved a friendly greeting. But when he and all his guests had gone into the house, there came the brothers and relations of the bride, who had been sent to rescue her. They locked the doors so that nobody could escape and set fire to the house, and the sorcerer and all his pack were burned to death.

The Devil
and His Three Golden Hairs

Once upon a time a poor woman gave birth to a little son and because he came into the world wrapped in his good-luck caul it was prophesied that in his fourteenth year he would marry the daughter of the king. Soon afterward the king happened to come to the village and nobody knew it was the king, and when he asked if there was any news, the people answered: "There was a child born here not long ago, wrapped in his good-luck caul. A child like that is lucky in everything he does, and it is prophesied that in his fourteenth year he will marry the daughter of the king." This prophecy vexed the king, who was a bad man. He went to the child's parents, acted pleasant, and said, "My poor people, let me have your child. I will provide for it." At first they refused but the stranger offered a large sum of money and they thought, The child is born lucky, so this can't help being for his own good. In the end they agreed and gave him the child.

The king put it into a box and rode until he came to a deep water, threw the box in, and thought, I have rid my daughter of one unexpected suitor. But the box did not sink, floated like a little ship, and not one droplet of water seeped inside; and so it floated on, and within two miles from the king's capital there stood a mill and the box caught in the weir. The miller's apprentice was standing near and luckily noticed it and pulled it out with a hook, expecting to find great treasure. But when he opened it up, there lay a beautiful boy, cheerful as could be. He brought him to the miller and his wife, who had no children and were happy and said, "Heaven has sent him to us as a gift." They took good care of the foundling and he grew up in God's grace.

One day there was a thunderstorm and the king happened to stop in the mill and asked the miller and his wife if that big boy was their son. "No," they answered, "he is a foundling. Fourteen years ago he floated into the weir in a box and our apprentice pulled him out of the water." And so the king knew it was none other than the good-luck child whom he had thrown into the river, and he said, "Good people, will you let the boy carry a letter to the queen for me? I will pay him two gold pieces." "Your majesty's word is our command," answered the couple, and told the boy to get ready. And so the king wrote the queen a letter which said, "As soon as the boy arrives with this letter, kill him and bury him and get it done before I come back."

With this letter the boy set out, but he lost his way and in the evening he came into a great forest. In the darkness he saw a light, went toward it, and came to a little hut. There was an old woman sitting by the fire all alone. When she saw the boy she was frightened and said, "Where do you come from and where are you going?" "I'm from the mill," answered he, "and have a letter to take to the queen, but I have lost my way in the forest and would like to spend the night here." "Poor boy," said the old woman, "you have fallen into a den of thieves. When they come home, they will murder you." "Let come who may," said the boy, "I am not afraid, but I am tired and can go no farther." He lay down on a bench and fell asleep. Soon after came the robbers and angrily asked what the strange boy was doing there. "Ah," said the old woman, "he's an innocent child who lost his way in the forest. I took him in for pity's sake. He is carrying a letter to the queen." The robbers tore the letter open and read it and it said that the boy was to be killed when he arrived. And so the hardhearted robbers felt sorry for the boy and their chief tore up the letter and wrote another which said that as soon as the boy arrived he should be married to the princess. Then they let him sleep quietly on his bench. In the morning when he woke up, they gave him the letter and showed him the way. When the queen received the letter and read it, she ordered a splendid wedding feast. The princess was married to the good-luck child, and because the boy was handsome and pleasant, lived with him happy and content.

After some time the king returned to his castle and saw that the prophecy had been fulfilled and the good-luck child had married his daughter. "How did this come about?" he asked. "I sent a very different command." And so the queen handed him the letter and said he could see for himself what it said. The king read the letter and saw that it had been changed. He asked the boy what had happened to the letter entrusted to him, and why he had brought a different one. "I wouldn't know," answered he. "It must have been exchanged at night in the forest, while I was asleep." In his fury the king said, "You can't have everything so easy! He who wants my daughter must go to hell and bring me three golden hairs from the devil's head. If you do as I ask, you shall keep my daughter." And this way he hoped to get rid of him once and for all. But the good-luck child answered, "I will go and fetch you the golden hairs. I am not afraid of the devil," said goodbye, and set out on his journey.

The road brought him to a big town and the watchman at the gate wanted to know all about him, what trade he followed and what he knew. "I know everything," answered the good-luck child. "Then you can do us a favor," said the watchman, "and tell us why the well that stands in the marketplace and used to overflow with wine has dried up and won't even give water now." "I will let you know," he answered. "Wait till I come back." And so he went on his way and came to another town and again the watchman at the gate wanted to know all about him, what trade he followed and what he knew. "I know everything," he answered. "Then you can do us a favor and tell us why a tree in our town used to bear golden apples and now won't even put out leaves." "I will let you know," he answered. "Wait till I come back." And so he went on and came to a deep river and had to cross over. The ferryman wanted to know all about him, what trade he followed and what he knew. "I know everything," he answered. "Then you can do me a favor," said the ferryman, "and tell me why I must keep rowing to and fro and nobody comes to relieve me." "I will let you know," he answered. "Wait till I come back."

When he got to the other side of the river, there was the entrance to hell. Inside, it was black and sooty. The devil wasn't home but there sat his grandmother in a great, wide easy chair. "What do you want here?" she asked, but didn't look so very mean. "I would like to have three golden hairs from the devil's head," he answered, "or I won't be allowed to keep my wife." "That's asking a lot," said she. "If the devil comes home and finds you, it'll be the end of you. But I'm sorry for you and will see if I can help you." She changed him into an ant and said, "Crawl into the fold of my skirt. You will be safe there." "Yes," said he, "that's fine as far as it goes, but there are also three things I would like to know: why a well that used to overflow with wine has dried up and won't even give water now; why a tree that used to bear golden apples won't even put out leaves; and why a ferryman must keep rowing to and fro and nobody comes to relieve him." "Those are hard questions," she answered, "but you just hold still and keep quiet and mark well what the devil says when I pull out his three hairs."

Around evening time the devil came home. No sooner had he entered than he noticed that the air was polluted. "I smell, I smell man's flesh," said he. "Something's not right here." Then he peeked in every corner and searched, but couldn't find anything. The grandmother scolded him. "I've just swept," said she, "and put everything in its place and there you go throwing things every which way. You've always got your nose full of human flesh. Sit down and eat your supper." When he had eaten and drunk he was tired, laid his head on his grandmother's lap, and told her to scratch his head for lice. It was not long before he dozed off with his mouth open and snored, and so the old woman took hold of a golden hair, pulled it out, and laid it next to her. "Ouch," howled the devil. "What are you doing!" "I had a bad dream," answered his grandmother, "and grabbed your hair." "Well, what did you dream?" asked the devil. "I dreamed that a well, in a marketplace, that used to overflow with wine had dried up, and now even water will not flow. I wonder what could be the matter?" "Ah, if they only knew!" answered the devil. "In the well, under a stone, sits a toad. If they killed it, the wine would soon flow again." The grandmother went on scratching for lice until he went back to sleep and snored so that the windows rattled. And so she pulled out the second hair. "Hey! What do you think you're doing?" the devil yelled in his fury. "Don't be angry with me," she answered. "I did it in my dream." "So what did you dream this time?" he asked. "I dreamed that in a kingdom there stood a fruit tree that used to bear golden apples and now it won't even put out leaves. I wonder what the cause might be." "Ah, if they only knew!" answered the devil. "On its roots there gnaws a mouse; if they killed it, the tree would soon bear golden apples again, but if it gnaws on, the tree will wither. But let me alone with your dreams. If you disturb my sleep once more, I'll box your ears." The grandmother talked him out of his bad temper and scratched for lice until he was asleep and snoring, then she took hold of the third golden hair and pulled it out. The devil shot into the air with a howl and would have done her some mischief, but she calmed him down again and said, "Who can help having bad dreams?" "Well, so what did you dream?" he asked, because he was curious. "I dreamed about a ferryman who complained that he must row to and fro and nobody comes to relieve him. I wonder why?" "Oh, the prize fool," an-

swered the devil. "If someone comes and wants to be rowed across, he must put the pole into his hand and then the other must row and he is free." And as the grandmother had now pulled out the three hairs and the three questions had been answered, she left the monster in peace and he slept till the break of day.

When the devil went off, the old woman took the ant out of the fold of her skirt and gave the good-luck child his human form again. "Here are the three golden hairs," said she. "You must have heard the devil's answer to your three questions." "I did," he said, "and remember every word." "Then that takes care of you," said she, "and you can be on your way." He thanked the old woman for her help and left hell in good spirits because he had been lucky and everything had turned out so well. When he came to the river, the ferryman was waiting for the promised answer. Said the good-luck child, "First row me across, and then I will tell you how to be free," and when he had got to the far shore he gave him the devil's advice: "When the next person comes to be ferried across, put the pole into his hand." He went on and came to the place where the unfruitful tree stood and here too the watchman wanted his answer. And so he told him what the devil said: "Kill the mouse that gnaws at its root and the tree will bear golden apples again," and the watchman thanked him and as a reward gave him two donkeys laden with gold and they followed on behind him. Finally he came to the city where the well had dried up and he told the watchman what the devil had said: "There is a toad that sits in the well, under a stone. You must find it and kill it and then the well will flow plentifully with wine." The watchman thanked him and gave him another pair of donkeys laden with gold.

Finally the good-luck child came home to his wife, who was heartily glad to see him again and to hear how well everything had gone. As for the king, the good-luck child brought him the devil's three golden hairs as he had wished, and when he saw the four donkeys laden with gold he was delighted and said, "All the conditions are now fulfilled and you may keep my daughter, but tell me, dear son-in-law, where does all this gold come from? This is an immense treasure." "I crossed a river," he answered, "and took it. It lies all over the shore instead of sand." "Oh, and can I go and get some too?" asked the king greedily. "As much as you want," he answered. "There is a ferryman on the river; let him row you across, so you can fill your sacks on the far side." Soon the avaricious king was on his way and when he came to the river he beckoned the ferryman to take him over to the other side. The ferryman let him get in and when they came to the far shore he put the pole into his hand, leaped out, and ran off, and the king has been rowing to and fro ever since, as a punishment for his sins.

"And is he rowing still?" "Of course! Who would take the pole away from him?"

The Fisherman and His Wife

Once upon a time there were a fisherman and his wife who lived together on the seashore in a pot, and every day the man would go and fish. And he fished and fished.

So once he was sitting there with his line, and kept looking into the clear water. And he sat and sat.

Then his line went to the bottom, way down under, and when he pulled it in, there on it was a big flounder. Then the flounder said to him: "Now just listen to me, fisherman. I beg you, let me live. I'm not a regular flounder, I'm an enchanted prince. What good will it do you to kill me? I wouldn't taste right anyway. Put me back in the water and let me swim off."

"Ah," said the man, "you didn't need to go on about it as much as all that—a flounder that can talk I'd let swim off anyway." With that he put it back in the clear water, and the flounder went to the bottom and left behind it a long streak of blood. Then the fisherman stood up and went back to his wife in the pot.

"Husband," said the wife, "didn't you catch anything today?"

"No," said the man. "I did catch a flounder, but it said it was an enchanted prince, so I let it go."

"You mean you didn't wish for anything?" said the wife.

"No," said the man. "What do I want to wish for?"

"My goodness," said the wife, "it's all wrong to have to keep living in a pot like this, that stinks so and is so disgusting; you could have wished for a little cottage for us, anyway. Go on back and call to it. Tell it we want to have a little cottage. It'll surely do that."

"Ah," said the man, "what do I want to go back for?"

"Why," said the woman, "you caught it, and you let it swim off again; it'll surely do that. Go on right this minute." The man didn't really want to. Still, though, he didn't want to go against his wife, so he went on down to the sea.

When he got there the sea was all green and yellow and not nearly so clear any more. So he went and stood by it and said:

> "Flounder, flounder in the sea,
>   Come to me, O come to me!
>   For my wife, good Ilsebill,
>   Wills not what I'd have her will."

Then the flounder came swimming up and said: "Well, what does she want then?"

"Ah," said the man, "I did catch you, so my wife says I ought to wish for something. She doesn't want to live in a pot any more; she'd like to have a cottage."

"Just go on back," said the flounder, "she's got it already."

Then the man went on home, and his wife wasn't sitting in the pot any more; but there stood a little cottage, and his wife was sitting in front of the door on a bench. Then his wife took him by the arm and said to him: "Just come on inside." Then they went on in, and inside the cottage there was a little hall, and a lovely little parlor and bedroom, with their bed in it, and a kitchen and pantry, all of the very best, with the finest sort of utensils hanging up in it, some tin and some brass, everything that ought to be there. And out behind there was a little yard, too, with hens and ducks and a little garden with vegetables and fruit trees. "See," said the wife, "isn't that nice?"

"Yes," said the man, "and let it stay that way; now we'll really be satisfied."

"We'll think about it," said the wife. Then they had a bite to eat and went to bed.

So things were fine for a week or two, then the wife said: "Listen, husband, this cottage is entirely too crowded, and the yard and the garden are just tiny; the flounder could perfectly well have given us a bigger house. Really I want to live in a great big stone castle: go on to the flounder, make it give us a castle."

"Ah, wife," said the man, "the cottage is plenty good

enough. What do we want to live in a castle for?"

"Nonsense!" said the wife. "Just you go on, the flounder can always do that."

"No, wife," said the man, "the flounder's just given us the cottage. I don't want to go back again, it might make the flounder mad."

"Go on anyway," said the wife. "It can do it all right, it'll be glad to. Just you go on!"

The man's heart was heavy, he didn't want to. He said to himself, "This isn't right," but just the same he went.

When he came to the sea, the water was all violet and dark blue and gray and not so green and yellow any more, but it was still calm. Then he went and stood by it and said:

> "Flounder, flounder in the sea,
> Come to me, O come to me!
> For my wife, good Ilsebill,
> Wills not what I'd have her will."

"Well, what does she want then?" said the flounder.

"Ah," said the man, pretty much upset, "she wants to live in a big stone castle."

"Just go on back, she's standing in front of the door," said the flounder.

Then the man went on back and thought he was going home, but when he got there, there stood a great big stone palace, and his wife was standing on the steps about to go in; she took him by the hand and said, "Come on inside." With that he went inside with her, and in the castle was a great big hall with a marble floor, and there were lots of servants, who opened the big doors, and the walls were all shiny and hung with beautiful tapestries, and in the rooms were chairs and tables all of pure gold, and crystal chandeliers were hanging from the ceiling, and all the rooms and chambers had carpets on the floor, and food and the very best wine were standing on all the tables, so that they almost broke under the weight. Behind the house was a big courtyard with stables for horses and cows, and the finest carriages; and there was a magnificent big garden besides, with the most beautiful flowers and fruit trees, and a park at least half a mile long, with deer and stags and hares and everything anyone could wish. Said the wife, "Now, isn't that fine?"

"Yes indeed," said the man, "and better let it stay that way, too—now we'll just live in this fine castle and be satisfied."

"We'll think about it," said the wife. "And now we'll sleep on it." With that they went to bed.

The next morning the wife woke up first. It was just day, and from her bed she looked out over the beautiful countryside that lay before her. The man was still stretching when she poked her elbow into his ribs and said: "Husband, get up and look out the window. Look, can't we be King over all that land? Go on to the flounder and tell him we want to be King."

"Ah, wife," said the man, "what do we want to be King for? I don't want to be King."

"Well," said the wife, "if you won't be King then I'll be King. Go on to the flounder; I want to be King."

"Ah, wife," said the man, "what do you want to be King for? I don't want to say that to the flounder."

"Why not?" said the woman. "Go on this minute, I've got to be King." Then the man went and was all upset that his wife wanted to be King. "It's not right, it just isn't right," thought the man. He didn't want to go, but just the same he went.

And when he got to the sea, the sea was all blackish gray and the water heaved up from underneath and stank just terribly. Then he went and stood by it and said:

> "Flounder, flounder in the sea,
> Come to me, O come to me!
> For my wife, good Ilsebill,
> Wills not what I'd have her will."

"Well, what does she want then?" said the flounder.

"Ah," said the man, "she wants to be King."

"Just go on back, she is already," said the flounder.

Then the man went on back, and when he came to the palace, the castle had got a lot bigger and had a great big tower with magnificent ornaments on it, and sentinels were standing in front of the gate, and there were lots of soldiers and drums and trumpets. And when he got inside the house, everything was made out of marble and pure gold, and there were velvet hangings and big golden tassels. Then the doors of the hall were opened, and there was the whole court, and his wife was sitting on a tall throne of gold and diamonds, and she had a great big golden crown on, and a scepter in her hand, made out of solid gold and covered with precious stones, and on both sides of her were standing six ladies-in-waiting in a row, every one of them a head shorter than the one before. Then he went and stood there and said: "Ah, wife, are you King now?"

"Yes," said the woman, "now I'm King." Then he just stood and looked at her, and when he'd looked at her that way a long time he said: "Ah, wife, how nice for you that you're King. Now we won't wish for another thing."

"No, husband," said the woman, and she was all excited, "the time just drags by. I can't stand it any longer. Go on to the flounder. I'm King, now I've got to be Emperor too."

"Ah, wife," said the man, "what do you want to be Emperor for?"

"Husband," said she, "go on to the flounder. I want to be Emperor."

"Ah, wife," said the man, "Emperors it can't make, I don't want to say that to the flounder; there's only one Emperor in the whole Empire. Emperors the flounder just can't make; it can't do it, it just can't do it."

"What!" said the woman, "I'm King, and you're my subject. Will you go on this minute! Go on this minute! If it can make Kings then it can make Emperors too. I want to be Emperor! Go on this minute!"

Then he had to go. But as the man went along, he got all frightened and thought to himself: "This gets worse and worse. Emperor is too shameless: at last the flounder is going to get sick of it."

With that he came to the sea. The sea was all black and thick, and began to boil up from underneath so that it threw up bubbles, and a whirlwind passed over it so that the water went round and round; and the man turned gray. Then he went and stood by it and said:

> "Flounder, flounder in the sea,
> Come to me, O come to me!
> For my wife, good Ilsebill,
> Wills not what I'd have her will."

"Well, what does she want then?" said the flounder. "Ah, flounder," said he, "my wife wants to be Emperor."

"Just go on back," said the flounder, "she is already."

Then the man went back, and when he got there the whole castle was made out of polished marble, with alabaster figures and golden ornaments. Soldiers were marching up and down in front of the door, and blowing trumpets and beating on drums and kettledrums; and inside the house there were barons and counts and dukes going back and forth just as if they were servants. They opened the doors for him, that were made out of solid gold. And when he went in, there sat his wife on a throne that was made out of one piece of gold and was at least two miles high; and she had on a great big golden crown that was three yards high and set with diamonds and carbuncles; in one hand she had the scepter and in the other the imperial apple, and on both sides of her, in two rows, were her life-guardsmen, each one smaller than the one before, from the biggest giant of all, who was two miles high, down to the littlest dwarf of all, who was just about as big as my little finger. And in front of her were standing lots of princes and dukes. Then the man went and stood among them and said: "Wife, are you Emperor now?"

"Yes," said she, "I'm Emperor."

Then he went and stood and took a good look at her, and when he'd looked at her that way a long time he said: "Ah, wife, how nice for you that you're Emperor."

"Husband," said she, "what are you standing there for? I'm Emperor now, but now I want to be Pope too. Go on to the flounder."

"Ah, wife," said the man, "what don't you want? You can't be Pope; in all Christendom there's only one Pope; it absolutely cannot make you Pope."

"Husband," said she, "I want to be Pope. Go on right away! This very day I've got to be Pope."

"No, wife," said the man, "I don't want to say that to it; this will never come to a good end; this is asking too much. The flounder can't make you Pope."

"Husband, what nonsense!" said the woman. "If it can make Emperors, then it can make Popes too. Go on this minute. I'm Emperor and you're my subject. Will you go on!"

Then he was frightened and went, but he felt all faint, and shivered and shook, and his knees and the calves of his legs trembled. And the wind blew over the land, and the clouds flew, and it got dark as night; the leaves fell from the trees, and the water surged and roared as if it were boiling, and the waves ran high and crashed down on the shore, and far off in the distance you could see ships firing distress signals and dancing up and plunging down on the waves. Yet in the middle of the sky there was still a little patch of blue, though all around on the horizon it was as red as though a tremendous thunderstorm were coming up. He went and stood there, all terrified and despairing, and said:

> "Flounder, flounder in the sea,
>   Come to me, O come to me!
>   For my wife, good Ilsebill,
>   Wills not what I'd have her will."

"Well, what does she want then?" said the flounder.

"Ah," said the man, "she wants to be Pope."

"Just go on back, she is already," said the flounder.

Then he went back, and when he got there, there was a great big church with nothing but palaces around it. Then he pushed his way through all the people, but inside everything was lit up with thousands upon thousands of candles, and his wife was all dressed in solid gold, and was sitting on a very much higher throne, and had three great big golden crowns on, and all around her was the greatest ecclesiastical pomp, and on both sides of her were standing two rows of candles, the biggest as thick and tall as the highest church tower, right down to the very smallest kitchen candle; and all the emperors and kings were on their knees before her, kissing her toe.

"Wife," said the man, and looked straight at her, "are you Pope now?"

"Yes," she said, "I'm Pope."

Then he went and stood and looked straight at her, and it was just as though he were looking into the bright sun. When he'd looked at her that way for a long time, he said: "Ah, wife, how nice for you that you're Pope."

But she sat there stiff as a poker, and didn't move or stir.

Then he said: "Wife, now be satisfied. Now you're Pope. Now you can't be any more."

"I'll think about it," said the woman. With that they both went to bed.

She wasn't satisfied, though. Her greed wouldn't let her sleep; she kept thinking every minute about what more she could be.

The man slept well and soundly—he'd walked a lot that day—but the woman just couldn't go to sleep, and threw herself from one side to the other the whole night through, and all the time she kept thinking what more she could be, but she just couldn't think of anything. As the sun was about to rise, and as she saw the red of dawn, she sat up in bed and stared straight out into it; and as she looked out the window, the sun came up. "Aha!" thought she, "couldn't I make the sun and the moon rise too?"

"Husband," said she, and poked him in the ribs with her elbow, "wake up, go to the flounder. I want to be like the good Lord."

The man was still half asleep, but it frightened him so that he fell out of bed. He thought he hadn't heard right, and rubbed his eyes and said: "Oh, wife, what are you saying?"

"Husband," said she, "if I can't make the sun and moon rise, and just have to watch the sun and moon

rise, I won't be able to bear it. I'll never again have another hour of peace, as long as I can't make the sun rise myself." Then she looked at him so terribly that a shudder went over him: "Go on this minute! I want to be like the good Lord!"

"Oh, wife," said the man, and fell on his knees before her, "the flounder can't do that. He can make Popes and Emperors—I beg you, think it over and stay Pope." Then she got so angry and spiteful that the hair flew all over her head, she tore open her nightgown, and kicked him, and shrieked: "I can't stand it, I can't stand it any longer! Will you go on!"

Then he pulled on his trousers and ran off like a madman. But outside a storm was raging so that he could hardly keep his feet: the houses and the trees fell, and the mountains shook, and the rocks rolled into the sea, and the sky was all pitch black, and there was thunder and lightning, and the sea came in black waves as high as steeples and mountains, and all of them had on top crests of white foam. Then he shouted, and he couldn't hear his own words:

"Flounder, flounder in the sea,
  Come to me, O come to me!
  For my wife, good Ilsebill,
  Wills not what I'd have her will."

"Well, what does she want then?" said the flounder.

"Ah," said he, "she wants to be like the good Lord."

"Just go on back, she's already sitting in the pot again."

And they're sitting there to this very day.

The Master Thief

One day an old man and his wife were sitting in front of their poor hut, resting from their work, when a magnificent carriage drawn by four black stallions came driving up and a richly dressed gentleman stepped out. The old peasant rose and went up to the gentleman and asked what he wished and if he could do anything for him. The stranger gave the old man his hand and said, "All I wish is to eat some country food. Cook me some potatoes the way you eat them and I will sit down at your table and enjoy them with you." The peasant

113

smiled and said, "You are a count or a duke or even a prince; noblemen do sometimes have such fancies, but you shall have what you want."

The woman went into the kitchen and began to wash and grate potatoes to make into dumplings the way peasants eat them. While she stood over her work the peasant said to the stranger, "Will your lordship come with me into the garden behind the house, where there is some work I have to finish." In the garden he had dug holes in which he wanted to plant trees. "Have you no children," asked the stranger, "who could help you with your work?" "No," answered the peasant. "I did have a son, but it is a long time now since he went out into the wide world. He was a spoiled child, clever and sharp, but never wanted to learn anything, and always full of mischief. In the end he ran away from home and I have not heard from him since." The old man took a young tree, put it into a hole, drove a stake in beside it, and when he had shoveled in the earth and tamped it firmly down, he took a rope made of straw and tied the stem to the stake, above, below, and in the middle. "Tell me," said the gentleman, "what about the crooked, knotted tree in the corner over there, that's almost bent to the ground. Why don't you tie it to a stake too, and make it grow strong?" The old man smiled and said, "You talk according to your lights, sir. One can tell that you have never done much gardening. That tree over there is old and gnarled and nothing can ever make it grow straight again. Trees have to be trained while they are young." "What about your son," said the stranger. "If you had trained him when he was still young, he would not have run off. By now he will have grown hard and gnarled too." "Very true," said the old man, "it is a long time since he went away; he must be changed." "Would you recognize him if he stood in front of you?" asked the stranger. "Probably not by his face," answered the peasant, "but he has a certain spot on his shoulder, a birthmark that looks like a bean." While he was speaking, the stranger took off his coat, bared his shoulder, and showed the peasant the bean. "God in heaven!" cried the old man. "You are my son indeed," and love for his child stirred in his heart. "But," added he, "how can you be my son? You have become a great gentleman and live in wealth

and luxury. How did you come by all this?" "Ah, dear
Father," answered the son, "the young tree was not tied
to the stake and has grown crooked; now it is too old
and will never be straight again. How I acquired all
this? Why, I have become a thief. But don't worry; I am
a master thief. For me there's neither lock nor bolt.
Whatever strikes my fancy is mine, but don't think I
steal like any common thief; I only take from the abundance of the rich; the poor are safe from me. I would
rather give them something than take something from
them, nor do I ever touch what I can get easily and
without trouble, cunning, and dexterity." "Ah, dear
son," said the father, "I don't like it, a thief is a thief.
You will come to a bad end." He led him in to his
mother, and when she heard that it was her son she
cried for joy; but when he told her that he had become
a master thief, two streams flowed down her face. In
the end she said, "Though he has become a thief, he
is still my son and my eyes have seen him again."

He sat down at the table with his parents and once
more ate the poor fare he had not eaten for so long. The
father said, "When his lordship the count in the castle

finds out who you are and how you earn your living, he won't hold you in his arms and rock you the way he did at your christening; you'll be rocking on the gallows." "Don't worry, dear Father. He can't hurt me; I know my trade. I will go to him myself before this day is done." When evening approached, the master thief got into his carriage and drove to the castle. The count received him courteously because he took him for a nobleman, but when the stranger made himself known, he paled and was silent for a while. In the end he said, "You are my godchild, so I will show mercy instead of justice and be lenient with you. Because you boast that you are a master thief, I will put your skill to the test, but if you do not pass, you shall tie the marriage knot with the ropemaker's daughter and the cawing of the crows will be your wedding song." "My lord," said the master, "choose the three most difficult tasks you can think of, and if I fail, do with me what you please." The count thought a few moments, and said, "Very well then, first you shall steal my favorite horse out of the stable. Next, when my wife and I have gone to sleep, you shall take the sheet from under us

117

without our noticing, as well as the wedding ring from my wife's finger. Third and lastly, you shall steal the parson and the sexton out of the church. Mark my words if you want to save your neck."

The master took off for the nearest town. Here he got an old peasant woman to sell him the clothes off her back and he put them on; then he colored his face brown and painted wrinkles on it so nobody could have known him. Finally he filled a small barrel with Hungarian wine into which he mixed a strong sleeping draught, put the barrel in his basket, took the basket on his back, and walked with careful, tottering steps to the count's castle. It was already dark when he arrived; he sat down on a stone in the yard and began to cough like a consumptive old woman and rubbed his hands as if he were freezing. In front of the door of the stable were soldiers lying around a fire. One of them noticed the woman and called to her, "Come closer, mother, and warm yourself. I bet you don't have a place to sleep, and will take one where you can get it." The old woman padded over, begged them to lift the basket off her back, and sat down with them at the fire. "Hey,

you old bag, what have you got in your barrel there?"
asked one. "A good swallow of wine," she answered.
"I earn my keep selling it, and for money and a kind
word I'll let you have some." "I'll take a taste," said
the soldier, and having drunk a glassful he cried, "When
the wine is good, I'd rather have a second glass," and
let her pour him another, and the rest followed his ex-
ample. "Hey, there, comrades," cried one to those who
sat inside the stable, "there's an old woman here selling
wine as old as herself. Have a swallow and it will warm
your stomachs better than a fire." The old woman
carried her barrel into the stable. The count's favorite
horse was saddled, one man sat mounted upon it, another grasped the reins in his hand, a third held on to
the tail. She poured what they asked for, until the well
ran dry. And it was not long before one let the reins
slip out of his hands and sank down and began to snore;
the other let go the tail and lay there and snored even
louder. The one in the saddle remained sitting but
doubled over until his head almost touched the horse's
neck, blowing through his mouth like a smith's bel-
lows. The soldiers outside had fallen asleep long since,

lay on the ground, and never stirred, as if they were
made of stone. When the master thief saw how luckily
everything had fallen out, he put a rope into the hand
of the one who had held the reins and gave the other
who had held the tail a bundle of straw. But what was
he to do with the one on the horse's back? He did not
want to throw him off, in case he woke and set up an
outcry. Then he had an idea: he unbuckled the girth of
the saddle, tied it to a couple of ropes that hung from
rings in the wall, and hoisted the sleeping rider, saddle
and all, into the air; then he wound the ropes around
the post and made them fast. He untied the horse from
its chain, but if he had ridden it across the stone paving of
the courtyard, the sound would have carried up to the
castle. So he first wrapped the horseshoes in old rags
and led it out carefully, swung himself up, and raced
away.

At daybreak the master galloped to the castle on
the stolen horse. The count, who had just got up, was
looking out of the window. "Good morning, your lordship," he called. "Here's the horse I stole out of your
stable. Take a look and see how sweetly your soldiers

sleep, and if you go inside the stable, you'll see how comfortable I have made your watchmen." The count had to laugh, then he said, "This once you were lucky, but the second time it won't go so well for you. I warn you, if I catch you thieving, I will treat you like a thief." In the evening, when the countess had gone to bed, she closed the hand with the wedding ring tightly, and the count said, "All the doors are locked and bolted. I will stay awake and wait for the thief, and if he climbs in the window, I will shoot him." The master thief, meanwhile, had gone out to the gallows in the dark, cut the poor sinner who hung there off the rope, set him on his back, and carried him to the castle. There he leaned a ladder against the bedroom window, took the dead man on his shoulders, and climbed up. When he was high enough for the dead man's head to appear in the window, the count, who was lying in wait on his bed, fired the pistol at him. The master let the poor sinner fall, leaped off the ladder himself, and hid in a corner. The moon lit the night so that the master could clearly see the count step out of the window onto the ladder, come down, and carry the dead man

121

into the garden. He began to dig a hole to put him in. Now, thought the thief, my moment has come; he stole nimbly out of his corner and climbed the ladder straight into the countess's bedroom. "Dear wife," he began, in the count's voice, "the thief is dead, but he was my godson and more rascal than villain. I don't want to disgrace him in public, and what's more I feel sorry for the poor parents. I will bury him in the garden before morning, so that this doesn't get about. Give me the bed sheet so I can wrap up the corpse and not stick him in the earth like a dog." The countess gave him the sheet. "You know what," the thief went on, "I'm suddenly overcome by generosity. Give me the ring too. The poor man put his life on the line, so let him take the ring into the grave with him." She would not oppose the count, and although she did not want to do it, took the ring from her finger and gave it to him. The thief went off with both things and got home safely before the count in the garden was finished with his gravedigging.

And didn't the count make a long face, next morning, when the master came and brought him sheet and ring.

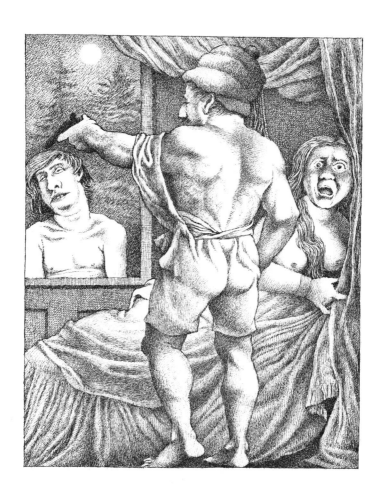

"Are you a sorcerer?" he said. "Who took you out of the grave I myself put you in? Who brought you back to life?" "It wasn't me you buried," said the thief, "but a poor sinner from the gallows," and he told him exactly what had happened, and the count had to grant that he was a clever and cunning thief. "But you're not done yet," he added. "You still have the third task to perform, and if you don't succeed there's no help for you." The master smiled and made no answer.

When night had fallen he came to the village church and had a long sack on his back, a bundle under his arm, and a lantern in his hand. In the sack were crabs and in the bundle wax candles. He sat down in the churchyard, took out a crab, and stuck a candle on its back, then he lighted it, put the crab on the ground, and let it crawl. He took out a second one, did the same, and went on until the sack was empty. Now he put on a long black gown that looked like a monk's robe and glued a gray beard on his chin. Finally, when he was quite unrecognizable, he took the sack in which he had brought the crabs, went into the church, and climbed the pulpit. Just then the church clock

125

struck twelve, and as the last chime was fading he cried out in a loud voice: "Hear ye that have sinned, the end of all things has come, the Day of Judgment is at hand! Hear, oh hear ye! Whoever wants to enter into the kingdom of heaven, let him creep into my sack. I am Peter who opens and closes the gates of heaven. See where out in the churchyard the dead wander, gathering their bones. Come, oh come and creep into my sack! The world is going under!" The yelling rang through the whole village. The parson and the sexton, who lived next to the church, were the first to hear, and when they saw the lights wandering all around the churchyard they knew there was something extraordinary going on and came into the church. For a while they listened to the sermon and then the sexton nudged the parson and said, "It wouldn't be a bad idea if we took the opportunity and got into heaven the easy way before the Day of Judgment comes." "Quite right," answered the parson, "that's just what I was thinking, so if you're inclined, let's go." "Yes," answered the sexton, "but you rank me, Parson. You get in first and I'll follow." And so the parson strode on ahead and climbed the pulpit, where the master opened the sack. The parson crawled into the sack and then came the sexton. The master quickly tied it up, grasped it by the knot, and dragged it down the pulpit stairs. As often as the heads of the two fools hit the steps, he cried, "Here we go over the mountains." In this way he pulled them through the village, and whenever they went through a puddle he cried, "Here we go through the wet clouds." And finally, when he was pulling them up the castle steps, he cried, "Now we're on the stair of heaven and will soon be in the forecourt." When he arrived at the top, he shoved the sack into the dovecot, and as the doves fluttered up he said, "Do you hear the angels rejoicing and clapping their wings?" and then he pushed the bolt and walked off.

The next morning he came to the count and told him that he had accomplished the third task as well and had stolen the parson and the sexton out of the church. "Where did you put them?" asked the count. "They are lying in a sack up in the dovecot, and think they are in heaven." The count climbed up and convinced himself that he had spoken the truth. When he

127

had let the parson and the sexton out of their prison, he said, "You are an archthief and you have won your case. This time you shall get away unscathed, but see that you take yourself off my land, because if I ever find you here again you can count on your elevation to the gallows." The archthief said goodbye to his parents, went back into the wide world, and has not been heard of since.

Brother Gaily

Once upon a time there was a great war, and when it was over, there was many a soldier got his discharge. Now Brother Gaily got his discharge too and nothing besides, except one small loaf of army bread and four pennies in cash; with this he set out on his way. But St. Peter had sat down by the wayside, disguised as a poor beggar, and when Brother Gaily came walking along, he asked him for alms. "Dear beggarman," answered Brother Gaily, "what shall I give you? I was a soldier and got my discharge and nothing besides, except this small loaf of army bread and four pennies cash. When that's gone I'll have to go begging just like you, but I will give you something." And so he divided the bread in four parts and gave one to the apostle and a penny as well. St. Peter thanked him, walked on, and in another disguise, as a different beggar, sat down in the soldier's path again, and when Brother Gaily came along, asked him for a gift as he had done the last time. Brother Gaily spoke as he had spoken before and gave him another quarter of the bread and another penny. St. Peter thanked him and walked on, but sat in his path for the third time disguised as another beggar and spoke to Brother Gaily, and Brother Gaily gave him the third quarter too, and the third penny. St. Peter thanked him and Brother Gaily walked on and had nothing left except one quarter of the bread and one penny. With this he went to an inn and ate the bread and bought himself a pennyworth of beer to go with it. When he had finished he went on his way, but St. Peter came walking toward him in the guise of a discharged soldier like himself and spoke to him. "Good morning, friend, can you spare a piece of bread and a penny for a drink?" "And where should I get it?" answered Brother Gaily. "They gave me my discharge and nothing besides, except one loaf of army bread and four pennies cash. On the road I met three beggars and gave each one a quarter of my bread and one penny. The last quarter I ate up at the inn and for the last penny bought myself a drink to go with it. Now I'm flat broke, and if you've got nothing left either, let's go begging together." "No," answered St. Peter, "it's not come to that yet. I am something of a doctor, so I'll manage to earn my keep." "Oh well," said Brother Gaily, "that's not a trade I know anything about, so I'll have to go begging by myself." "Why don't you come along with me, then," said St. Peter. "And if I earn anything, you shall have half." "That's fine with me," said Brother Gaily. And they went on their way together.

Now they came to a farmhouse and heard a tremendous moaning and crying, so they went inside and there lay the man, deathly sick and ready to pass on, and the wife was weeping and wailing noisily. "Stop your weeping and wailing," said St. Peter, "I will make your husband well again," took an ointment out of his pocket, and cured the sick man in the wink of an eye so that he stood right up, perfectly healthy. Said the husband and wife in their great joy, "How shall we repay you! What can we give you?" But St. Peter would not take anything, and the more the peasants offered, the more he declined. Brother Gaily nudged St. Peter and said, "Go on, take something, we can do with it." In the end the peasant's wife brought a lamb, saying this he must take, but St. Peter did not want it. Brother Gaily poked him in the ribs and said, "Why the devil don't you take it, you blockhead. We can do with it." And so finally St. Peter said, "All right, I'll take the lamb but I won't carry it. If you want it, you carry it." "Don't you worry about that," said Brother Gaily, "I'll carry it all right," and took it on his shoulders. And so they went on their way and came to a forest, and the lamb was getting too heavy for Brother Gaily and he was hungry, so he said, "Look, here's a nice place, here's where we can cook the lamb and eat." "All right," answered St. Peter, "only I'm no good at cooking. If you want to cook, here is a kettle. I'll walk up and down until it is done. But you must not start eating before I come. I will be back in good time." "You go along then," said Brother Gaily. "I'm a good cook, I'll do it." And so St. Peter walked off and Brother Gaily slaughtered the lamb, lit a fire, threw the meat into the kettle, and let it cook. But the lamb was already done and still the apostle hadn't come back, and so Brother Gaily took it out of the kettle, cut it up, and found the heart. "That's supposed to be the best part," said he and tasted it and in the end he ate it. Finally St. Peter came back and said, "You may eat the whole lamb by yourself, all I want is the heart. Give it to me." So Brother Gaily took knife and fork and made as if he were searching busily through the meat but could not find the heart. In the end, without more ado, he said, "It's not here." "It's not? Well then, where could it be?" said the apostle. "How should I know?" answered Brother Gaily. "But look what fools we are, both of us, looking for the heart of a lamb, and it doesn't occur to either of us! A lamb doesn't even have a heart!" "Really?" said St. Peter. "That's news to me. Every animal has a heart. Why shouldn't a lamb have one?" "No, honestly, brother, a lamb doesn't have a heart. You think about it and it'll come to you; it just doesn't." "All right, let it go," said St. Peter, "if there's no heart, I don't need any lamb; you can eat it by yourself." "Well, then what I can't finish I'll take along in my knapsack," said Brother Gaily, ate up half the lamb, and put the rest into his knapsack.

And so they went on their way and St. Peter made a great river flow right across their path and they had to cross over. Said St. Peter, "You go on ahead." "No," answered Brother Gaily, "you go ahead," and thought, If the water is too deep for him, I'm staying here. So St. Peter strode across and the water barely reached to his knee. Now Brother Gaily wanted to cross too, but the river became deeper until it rose to his neck, and he cried out and said, "Brother, help me!" Said St. Peter, "Will you confess that you ate the heart of the lamb?" "No," answered Brother Gaily, "I didn't eat it." And so the water became still deeper and rose to his mouth. "Help me, brother," cried the soldier. And again St. Peter said, "Will you confess that you ate the heart of the lamb?" "No," he answered, "I did not." St. Peter didn't want to let him drown, made the water fall, and

helped him across.

And so they went on and came to a kingdom where they heard that the king's daughter lay sick to death. "Now then, brother," the soldier said to St. Peter, "here's a windfall for you and me! If we cure this one, we're made men for all eternity." But St. Peter didn't move fast enough for him. "Come on, shake a leg, old friend," he said, "so that we get there before it's too late." But St. Peter just walked slower, and the more Brother Gaily drove and pushed him, the slower he walked, until in the end they heard that the king's daughter was dead. "There!" said Brother Gaily, "all because of this sleepy way you walk." "Don't worry," answered St. Peter, "I can do better than make the sick well, I can bring the dead back to life." "Well, in that case!" said Brother Gaily. "That's good enough for me. But it's got to earn us half the kingdom at the very least!" And so they came into the royal palace, where everyone was in deep mourning. St. Peter told the king he would bring his daughter back to life and so he was taken to her and he said, "Bring me a kettle of water," and when they had brought it he asked everyone to leave and only Brother Gaily was allowed to stay with him. Then he cut the dead girl in pieces and threw the pieces into the water, lit a fire under the kettle, and boiled them. And when all the flesh had fallen off, he took out the beautiful white bones and laid them on a table and put them in their natural order, and when that was done he came and stood before them and said three times, "In the name of the most Holy Trinity, you who are dead, arise," and at the third time the princess rose alive and healthy and beautiful. Now the king was overjoyed and said, "Ask for your reward, and if it's half my kingdom, I will give it to you." But St. Peter said, "I ask for nothing." Oh, you everlasting fool, thought Brother Gaily to himself, poked his companion in the ribs, and said, "Don't be a blockhead, if you don't want something, I can certainly do with it." St. Peter wouldn't take anything, but the king saw how very much the other wanted a reward and had the treasurer fill his knapsack with gold.

And so they went on their way and came to a forest, and St. Peter said, "Now let us divide up the gold." "Yes, let's do that," answered Brother Gaily, and so St.

Peter divided up the gold and divided it into three parts. Thought Brother Gaily, There he goes again, he must have a screw loose somewhere, making three parts when there are only two of us. But St. Peter said, "I have divided it exactly, one part for me, one part for you, and one part for the one who ate the heart of the lamb." "Oh, that was me," answered Brother Gaily quickly and swept the money into his pocket. "I ate it, honestly I did." "How can that be," said St. Peter, "when a lamb doesn't have a heart." "Oh, come on, brother, where did you get that idea! Of course a lamb has a heart, just like every other animal. Why shouldn't a lamb have one?" "All right, let it go," said St. Peter, "and you can keep the gold for yourself, only I'm not staying with you any longer. I'll go on alone." "Just as you like, old friend," answered the soldier. "Take care!"

And so St. Peter took a different road, but Brother Gaily thought, Just as well that he's trotting off. Saints alive, what a character! Now he had plenty of money, to be sure, but did not know how to handle it; he squandered it, gave it away, and after a time had nothing again. And so he came into a country where he heard that the king's daughter had died. Hello, thought he, this is going to be something. I'll make that girl come back to life and make them pay through the nose. So he went to the king and offered to bring the dead princess back to life. Now the king had heard about a discharged soldier traveling through the land bringing dead people back to life and thought Brother Gaily might be the man, but because he did not trust him he first asked his counselors, and they said he might as well take the chance, his daughter was dead anyway. And so Brother Gaily had them bring a kettle of water, made everybody go outside, cut the princess into pieces, threw them in the water, and lit a fire under it, just as he had watched St. Peter do. The water began to boil and the flesh fell off the bones and he took the bones out and put them on the table, only he didn't know the order in which they must lie and laid them every which way, back to front. Then he went and stood before them and said, "In the name of the most Holy Trinity, you who are dead, arise," and said it three times, but the bones didn't move and so he said it three more times, in vain. "Arise, you silly goose, if you know what's good for you!" he said. And when he had spoken thus, St. Peter in his former guise of a discharged soldier suddenly came walking in through the window and said, "You wicked man, what do you think you're doing? How can the dead princess arise when you have thrown her bones in such a jumble." "I did the best I could, old friend," answered he. "This time I will help you out of your trouble, but I tell you one thing. If you ever do anything like this again, it will be a bad day's work for you, nor may you request or accept the smallest tittle from the king." And so St. Peter laid the bones in the right order, said three times, "In the name of the most Holy Trinity, you who are dead, arise," and the princess arose and was healthy and beautiful as ever, and St. Peter went back out through the window. Brother Gaily was glad that everything had gone off so well, but it annoyed him that he was not to be allowed to take the reward. That fellow must have some sort of bee in his bonnet, he thought; what he gives with one hand he takes away with the other. It doesn't make any sense. Now the king offered Brother Gaily whatever he wanted, but he couldn't take anything. Nevertheless, by hints and cunning, he brought it about that the king had his knapsack filled with gold, and so he went on his way. As he came out of the town, St. Peter was standing before the gates and said, "Now look, what sort of a man are you! Didn't I forbid you to accept anything and here you've got a knapsack full of gold." "How can I help what someone puts in?" answered Brother Gaily. "I want to tell you one thing: don't you ever do anything like that again or it will be the worse for you!" "Don't you worry, brother! Now I've got all this gold, why should I spend my time washing bones?" "Yes," said St. Peter, "that gold will last you a long time! So that you will not walk in forbidden paths hereafter, I'll give your knapsack this magic power: whatever you wish into it shall be in it. Goodbye. You won't see me again." "Goodbye to you too," said Brother Gaily, and thought, Good riddance, you strange bird! I won't go running after you, that's for sure!

As for the power bestowed upon his knapsack, he never gave it a thought.

Brother Gaily wandered around with his gold and

splurged, and wasted it like the first time, and when he had nothing left except four pennies, he was walking past an inn and thought, The money must go, and ordered three pennyworth of wine and one pennyworth of bread. As he sat drinking, the smell of roast goose came into his nostrils. Brother Gaily peered and peeked and saw that the innkeeper had two geese in the oven. And it came to him how his companion had said that everything he wished into his knapsack would be in it. Hello, he thought, you've got to try it with these geese. And so he left, but when he was outside the door he said, "All right then, I wish the two roast geese out of the oven into my knapsack," and then he unbuckled it and looked inside and there were the two geese. "That's the way!" said he, "now I am a made man," went and sat down in a meadow, took out his roast, and was tucking in when along came two journeymen and looked with hungry eyes at the goose that was still untouched. Thought Brother Gaily, You have enough with one, called the two lads over, and said, "Here, you take the goose and eat to my health." They thanked him, carried it to the inn, ordered a half bottle of wine and a loaf of bread, unpacked the goose they had been given, and began to eat. The innkeeper's wife watched them, called her husband, and said, "Those two are eating a goose. Go, take a look and see if it isn't one of ours from the oven." The host ran and looked and the oven was empty. "Oh, you pack of thieves, you want to eat your geese good and cheap, do you! Pay up, or I'll tan your hides with birch juice." The two lads said, "We are no thieves. There was a discharged soldier in the meadow, he gave us the goose." "Don't you cock your snook at me! That soldier was in here and walked out this door an honest man. I had my eye on him. You are the thieves and you're going to pay up." But as they could not pay, he took a birch switch and beat them all the way out the door.

Brother Gaily went on his way and came to a village and there stood a splendid castle and not far from it a miserable inn and here he asked for a night's lodging, but the innkeeper turned him away, saying, "There's no more room, the house is full of gentry." "That's strange," said Brother Gaily. "Why do they come here when there's such a splendid castle nearby?" "That would be something," answered the innkeeper, "to spend the night there! No one who tried has ever come back alive." "If others have tried," said Brother Gaily, "so will I!" "Let it alone," said the innkeeper, "or it will cost you your head." "I don't lose my head so easily," said Brother Gaily. "Give me the key and plenty of food and drink to take with me." And so the innkeeper gave him the key, and food and drink, and Brother Gaily took it to the castle with him, enjoyed a good meal, and when he became sleepy, lay down on the ground because there was no bed. Soon he was asleep, but in the middle of the night he was roused by a great noise. When he had fully woken he saw that there were nine hideous devils in the room who had made a ring about him and were dancing all around. Said Brother Gaily, "Go ahead, dance all you want, only don't any of you come too near." But the devils kept crowding closer and almost trod on his face with their nasty feet. "Take it easy there, you devilish ghosts," said he, but they carried on worse than ever. And so Brother Gaily got angry and cried, "Now then, I'm going to get me a little peace and quiet here," took hold of a chair leg, and hit out at them. But nine devils against one soldier are too many, and while he was hitting the ones in front, the ones behind grabbed him and pulled him mercilessly by the hair. "Devil's pack!" cried he, "now I've had enough. Just you wait. Into my knapsack, all nine of you!" Whoosh! and they were inside it and he buckled it and threw it in a corner, and all of a sudden there was quiet and Brother Gaily lay down and slept till the bright morning. Now the innkeeper and the nobleman who owned the castle came to see what had happened to him. When they found him well and in good spirits, they were amazed and asked, "Didn't the ghosts bother you?" "Not a bit of it," answered Brother Gaily. "I've got all nine of them inside my knapsack. You can come back and live quietly in your castle. Nobody is going to haunt any longer." And so the nobleman thanked him and gave him rich presents, begged him to remain in his service, and promised to provide for him as long as he lived. "No," answered he, "I'm used to wandering and need to be on the move." And so Brother Gaily went on his way, and went into a smithy, laid the knapsack with the nine devils inside it on the anvil, and asked the smith and his apprentices to go ahead and hammer. They wielded their great hammers with all their might. The devils screeched piteously, and when he opened the knapsack later, eight of them were dead, but one who had sat in a fold and was still alive slipped out and fled back to hell.

After that, Brother Gaily wandered around the world yet a long while, and I could tell you many more stories if I knew them, but finally he got old and began to think of his end. And so he went to a hermit who was known as a pious man and said, "I'm tired of wandering and want to see about getting into the heavenly kingdom." The hermit answered, "There are two paths. One is wide and pleasant and leads to hell; the other is rough and narrow and leads to heaven." Then I'd be a fool, thought Brother Gaily, if I took the rough and narrow one. He set out, walked the wide and pleasant path, and finally came to a big black gate, and it was the gate of hell. Brother Gaily knocked and the gatekeeper peered out to see who it might be. But when he saw Brother Gaily he took fright, for he happened to be the very ninth devil who had been inside the knapsack and got away with a black eye. He quickly pushed the bolt, ran off to the chief of devils, and said, "There's a fellow outside with a knapsack who wants to come in, but it's as much as your life is worth not to let him, or he will wish all hell into his knapsack. He once had me horribly hammered in it." And so they called to Brother Gaily outside to go away, he couldn't come in. If they don't want me here, he thought, I'll see if I can find accommodation in heaven. I've got to stay somewhere. And so he turned around and walked on until he came to the door of heaven and here he knocked too. St. Peter happened to be sitting there, keeping watch at the gate. Brother Gaily knew him right away and thought, There's your old friend. Now you'll be all right. But St. Peter said, "I do believe you want to get into heaven." "Let me in, brother, I've got to stay somewhere. If they had taken me into hell, I wouldn't be here." "No," said St. Peter, "you can't come in." "All right, if you won't let me in, take your knapsack back, I don't want anything of yours," said Brother Gaily. "Give it to me, then," said St. Peter, and so Brother

Gaily pushed the knapsack through the railings into heaven and St. Peter took it and hung it up beside him on his chair, but Brother Gaily said, "Now I wish myself inside my knapsack." Whoosh! and he was inside and that's how he got to heaven and St. Peter had to let him stay.

The Goblins

Once there was a mother and the goblins had stolen her child out of the cradle. In its place they laid a changeling with thick head and staring eyes who did nothing but eat and drink. In her misery, the woman went to ask her neighbor for advice. The neighbor told her to take the changeling into the kitchen, set him on the hearth, light a fire, and boil water in two eggshells. This would make the changeling laugh, and when a changeling laughs, that's the end of him.

The woman did just what the neighbor told her, and

as she was putting the eggshells full of water on the fire, the blockhead said:

> "Now am I as old
>   As the western woods
>   But never heard it told
>   that people cook water in eggshells,"

and he began to laugh and as he laughed there suddenly came a lot of little goblins who brought the right child and set it on the hearth and took their friend away with them.

Hansel and Gretel

Once upon a time, on the edge of a great forest, there lived a poor woodcutter with his wife and his two children. The boy was named Hansel and the girl was named Gretel. The family had little enough to eat, and once when there was a great famine in the land the man could no longer even get them their daily bread. One night, lying in bed thinking, in his worry he kept tossing and turning, and sighed, and said to his wife: "What is going to become of us? How can we feed our poor children when we don't even have anything for ourselves?"

"You know what, husband?" answered the wife. "The first thing in the morning we'll take the children out into the forest, to the thickest part of all. There we'll make them a fire and give each of them a little piece of bread; then we'll go off to our work and leave them there alone. They won't be able to find their way back home, and we'll have got rid of them for good."

"No, wife," said the man, "I won't do it. How could I have the heart to leave my children alone in the forest —in no time the wild beasts would come and tear them to pieces."

"Oh, you fool!" said she. "Then all four of us will starve to death—you may as well start planing the planks for our coffins," and she gave him no peace until he agreed. "I do feel sorry for the poor children, though," said the man.

The two children hadn't been able to go to sleep either, they were so hungry, and they heard what their stepmother said to their father. Gretel cried as if her heart would break, and said to Hansel: "We're as good as dead." "Ssh! Gretel," said Hansel, "don't you worry, I'll find some way to help us." And as soon as the old folks had gone to sleep, he got up, put on his little coat, opened the bottom half of the door, and slipped out. The moon was shining bright as day, and the white pebbles that lay there in front of the house glittered like new silver coins. Hansel stooped over and put as many as he could into his coat pocket. Then he went back in again, and said to Gretel: "Don't you feel bad, dear little sister! You just go to sleep. God will take care of us." Then he lay down in his bed again.

The next morning, before the sun had risen, the woman came and woke the two children: "Get up, you lazy creatures, we're going to the forest and get wood." Then she gave each of them a little piece of bread and said: "There is something for your dinner, but don't you eat it before, because it's all you're going to get." Gretel put the bread in her apron, since Hansel had the pebbles in his pocket. Then they all started out together on the way to the forest. After they had been walking a little while Hansel stopped and looked back at the house, and did it again and again. His father said: "Hansel, what are you looking at? What are you hanging back there for? Watch out or you'll forget your legs."

"Oh, Father," said Hansel, "I'm looking at my little white pussycat that's sitting on the roof and wants to say goodbye to me."

The wife said: "Fool, that's not your pussycat, that's the morning sun shining on the chimney." But Hansel hadn't been looking back at the cat—every time he'd stopped he'd dropped onto the path one of the white pebbles from his pocket.

When they came to the middle of the forest the father said: "Now get together some wood, children! I'll light you a fire, so you won't be cold." Hansel and Gretel pulled together brushwood till it was as high as a little mountain. The wood was lighted, and when the flames were leaping high, the woman said: "Now lie down by the fire, children, and take a rest, we're going into the forest to cut wood. When we're finished we'll come back and get you."

Hansel and Gretel sat by the fire, and when noon came they each ate their little piece of bread. And since they heard the blows of the ax, they thought their father was near. But it wasn't the ax, it was a branch that he'd fastened to a dead tree so that the wind would blow it back and forth. And when they'd been sitting there a long time, they got so tired that their eyes closed, and they fell fast asleep. When at last they woke up, it was pitch black. Gretel began to cry, and said: "Now how will we ever get out of the forest?" But Hansel comforted her: "Just wait awhile till the moon comes up, then we'll be able to find our way." And when the full moon had risen, Hansel took his little sister by the hand and followed the pebbles, that glittered like new silver coins and showed them the way.

They walked the whole night through, and just as the day was breaking they came back to their father's house. They knocked on the door, and when the woman opened it and saw that it was Hansel and Gretel, she said: "You bad children, why did you sleep so long in the forest? We thought you weren't coming back at all." But the father was very glad, for it had almost broken his heart to leave them behind alone.

Not long afterwards there was again a famine throughout the land, and the children heard their mother saying to their father in bed one night: "Everything's eaten again. We've only a half a loaf left, and that will be the end of us. The children must go. We'll take them deeper into the forest, so that this time they won't find their way back; it's our only chance." The man's heart was heavy, and he thought: "It would be better for you to share the last bite of food with your children." But the woman wouldn't listen to what he had to say, but scolded him and reproached him. If you say "A" then you have to say "B" too, and since he had given in the first time, he had to give in the second time too.

But the children were still awake, and had heard what was said. As soon as the old folks were asleep, Hansel got up again to go out and pick up pebbles as he'd done the time before, but the woman had locked the door, and Hansel couldn't get out. He comforted his little sister, though, and said: "Don't cry, Gretel, but just go to sleep. The good Lord will surely take care of us."

Early in the morning the woman came and got the children out of their beds. She gave them their little piece of bread, but this time it was even smaller than the time before. On the way to the forest Hansel broke up the bread in his pocket, and often would stop and scatter the crumbs on the ground. "Hansel, what are you stopping and looking back for?" said the father. "Come on!"

"I'm looking at my little pigeon that's sitting on the roof and wants to say goodbye to me," answered Hansel.

"Fool," said the woman, "that isn't your pigeon, that's the morning sun shining on the chimney." But Hansel, little by little, scattered all the crumbs on the path.

The woman led the children still deeper into the forest, where they'd never been before in all their lives. Then there was again a great fire made, and the mother said: "Just sit there, children, and if you get tired you can take a nap. We're going into the forest to cut wood, and this evening when we're finished we'll come and get you."

When it was noon, Gretel shared her bread with Hansel, who'd scattered his along the way. Then they fell asleep, and the afternoon went by, but no one came to the poor children. They didn't wake until it was pitch black, and Hansel comforted his little sister, and said: "Just wait till the moon comes up, Gretel, then we'll see the bread crumbs I scattered. They'll show us the way home." When the moon rose they started out, but they didn't find any crumbs, for the many thousands of birds that fly about in the fields and in the forest had picked them all up. Hansel said to Gretel: "Surely we'll find the way." But they didn't find it. They walked all that night and all the next day, from morning to evening, but they never did get out of the forest. And they were so hungry, for they'd had nothing to eat but a few berries they found on the ground. And when they got so tired that their legs wouldn't hold them up any longer, they lay down under a tree and fell asleep.

By now it was already the third morning since they'd left their father's house. They started to go on again, but they kept getting deeper and deeper into the forest, and unless help came soon they must die of hunger. When it was noon, they saw a beautiful snow-white bird, sitting on a bough, who sang so beautifully that they stood still and listened to him. As soon as he had finished he spread his wings and flew off ahead of them, and they followed him till they came to a little house. The bird perched on the roof of it, and when they got up close to it they saw that the little house was made of bread and the roof was made of cake; the windows, though, were made out of transparent sugar-candy.

"We'll get to work on that," said Hansel, "and have a real feast. I'll eat a piece of the roof. Gretel, you can eat some of the window—that will taste sweet!" Hansel reached up and broke off a little of the roof, to see how it tasted, and Gretel went up to the windowpane and nibbled at it. Then a shrill voice called out from inside the house:

> "Nibble, nibble, little mouse,
> Who is gnawing at my house?"

The children answered:

> "It is not I, it is not I—
> It is the wind, the child of the sky,"

and they went on eating without stopping. The roof tasted awfully good to Hansel, so he tore off a great big piece of it, and Gretel pushed out a whole round windowpane, and sat down and really enjoyed it.

All at once the door opened, and a woman as old as the hills, leaning on crutches, came creeping out. Hansel and Gretel were so frightened that they dropped what they had in their hands. But the old woman just nodded her head and said: "My, my, you dear children, who has brought you here? Come right in and stay with me. No harm will befall you." She took both of them by the hand and led them into her little house. Then she set nice food before them—milk and pancakes with sugar, apples and nuts. After that she made up two beautiful white beds for them, and Hansel and Gretel lay down in them and thought they were in heaven.

But the old woman had only pretended to be so friendly; really she was a wicked witch who lay in wait for children, and had built the house of bread just to lure them inside. When one came into her power she would kill it, cook it, and eat it, and that would be a real feast for her. Witches have red eyes and can't see far, but they have a keen sense of smell, like animals, so that they can tell whenever human beings get near. As Hansel and Gretel had got close the witch had given a wicked laugh, and had said mockingly: "Now I've got them. This time they won't get away."

Early in the morning, before the children were awake,

she was already up, and when she saw both of them fast asleep and looking so darling, with their rosy fat cheeks, she muttered to herself: "That will be a nice bite!" Then she seized Hansel with her shriveled hands and shut him up in a little cage with a grating in the lid, and locked it; and scream as he would, it didn't help him any. Then she went to Gretel, shook her till she woke up, and cried: "Get up, you lazy creature, fetch some water and cook your brother something good. He has to stay in the cage and get fat. As soon as he's fat I'll eat him." Gretel began to cry as if her heart would break, but it was all no use. She had to do what the wicked witch told her to do.

Now the finest food was cooked for poor Hansel, but Gretel got nothing but crab shells. Every morning the old woman would creep out to the cage and cry: "Hansel, put your finger out so I can feel whether you are getting fat." But Hansel would put out a bone, and the old woman's eyes were so bad that she couldn't tell that, but thought it was Hansel's finger, and she just couldn't understand why he didn't get fat.

When four weeks had gone by and Hansel still was as

thin as ever, she completely lost patience, and was willing to wait no longer. "Come on, Gretel, hurry up and get some water! Whether he's fat or whether he's thin, tomorrow I'll kill Hansel and cook him."

Oh, how the poor little sister did grieve as she had to get the water, and how the tears ran down her cheeks! "Dear Lord, help us now!" she cried out. "If only the wild beasts in the forest had eaten us, then at least we'd have died together."

"Stop making all that noise," said the old woman. "It won't help you one bit."

Early the next morning Gretel had to go out and fill the kettle with water and light the fire. "First we'll bake," said the old woman. "I've already heated the oven and kneaded the dough." She pushed poor Gretel up to the oven, out of which the flames were already shooting up fiercely. "Crawl in," said the witch, "and see whether it's got hot enough for us to put the bread in." And when Gretel was in, she'd close the oven and Gretel would be baked, and then she'd eat her too. But Gretel saw what she was up to, and said: "I don't know how to. How do I get inside?"

"Goose, goose!" cried the witch, "the oven is big enough—why, look, I can even get in myself," and she scrambled up and stuck her head in the oven. Then Gretel gave her a push, so that she fell right in, and Gretel shut the door and fastened the bolt. Oh, then she began to howl in the most dreadful way imaginable, but Gretel ran away, and the wicked witch burned to death miserably.

But Gretel ran to Hansel as fast as she could, opened the cage, and cried: "Hansel, we are saved! The old witch is dead!" Hansel sprang out like a bird from its cage when the door was opened. How they did rejoice, and throw their arms around each other's necks, and dance around and kiss each other! And since there wasn't anything to fear, now, they went into the witch's house, and in every corner of it stood chests of pearls and precious stones. "These are even better than pebbles," said Hansel, and stuck into his pocket as many as he could; and Gretel said, "I'll take some home too," and filled her apron full.

"Now it's time for us to go. We must get out of this enchanted forest," said Hansel. But when they'd walked for a couple of hours they came to a wide lake. "We can't get across," said Hansel. "There isn't a plank or a bridge anywhere."

"There isn't a boat either," answered Gretel, "but there's a little white duck swimming over there—if I ask her to, she will help us over." Then she cried:

> "They haven't a bridge and they haven't a plank,
> Hansel and Gretel are out of luck.
> Please take us across to the other bank
> And we'll thank you so, you little white duck!"

The duck did come over to them, and Hansel sat down on her back and told his sister to sit behind him. "No," answered Gretel, "it would be too heavy for the little duck. She can take us over one at a time."

The good little bird did that, and when they were happily on the other side, and had gone on for a little while, they came to a wood that kept looking more and more familiar, and at last, in the distance, they saw their father's house. Then they started to run, burst into the living room, and threw themselves on their father's neck. Since he had left the children in the forest he had

167

not had a single happy hour. His wife, though, had died. Gretel shook out her apron, and pearls and precious stones rolled all over the room, and Hansel threw down out of his pocket one handful after another. All their troubles were at an end and they lived together in perfect happiness. My tale is done, there is no more, but there's a mouse upon the floor—the first of you that catches her can make a great big cap from her fur.

The Juniper Tree

· II ·

THE JUNIPER TREE
and Other Tales from Grimm

Selected by Lore Segal and Maurice Sendak

Translated by Lore Segal
With four tales translated by Randall Jarrell

Pictures by Maurice Sendak

· II ·

Farrar, Straus and Giroux · New York

The Tales

The Pictures

VOLUME II

The Juniper Tree

·II·

The Frog King, or Iron Henry

In the old days, when wishing still helped, there lived a king and all his daughters were beautiful, but the youngest was so beautiful that even the sun, which has seen so much, marveled every time it shone into her face. Near the king's castle lay a great, dark forest and in the forest, under an old linden tree, there stood a well. Now on the days when it was very hot the princess would go out into the forest and sit at the edge of the cool well and if time hung heavy on her hands she took a golden ball, threw it in the air, and caught it, and it was her favorite plaything.

It happened once that the princess's golden ball did not fall into her outstretched hand but slipped past, struck the ground, made straight for the water, and rolled in. The princess followed it with her eyes but the ball disappeared, and the well was deep, so deep that you couldn't see the bottom, and she began to cry and kept crying louder and louder and could not stop. And as she sat wailing, someone called, "What's the matter, Princess? The way you howl would melt the heart of a stone!" The princess looked around to see who it could be and saw a frog sticking his thick, ugly head out of the water. "Oh, it's you, you old puddle-splasher," said she. "I'm crying because my golden ball has fallen into the well." "Well, don't cry any more," answered the frog, "I can help you. What will you give me if I bring back your toy?" "Anything you want, dear frog," said she, "my dresses, my pearls and all my jewels, and the gold crown on my head as well." "I don't care anything about your dresses, your pearls and jewels, or your golden crown, but if you will promise to love me best and play with me, and let me be your dearest friend, and sit beside you at the table, eat off your golden plate, drink from your cup, and sleep in your bed with you, I will climb down and bring back your golden ball." "Yes, yes, I promise everything, only bring me my ball," said she, thinking, The silly frog! What nonsense he does talk; he sits here in the water with his own kind and croaks, and can never be friends with real people.

When the frog had obtained her promise, he put his head in the water, sank down, and after a little while came paddling back up with the ball in his mouth and threw it on the grass. The princess was overjoyed to see her pretty toy, picked it up, and ran away. "Wait for me, wait for me," cried the frog. "Take me with you, I can't run so fast," but what was the good of his croaking after her as loud as he could? She would not hear him but hurried home and soon forgot the poor frog, who had to climb back into his well.

The next day, as she was sitting at the table with the king and all the court, and was eating from her golden plate, there came something crawling, splash, splash, up the marble stair. When it arrived at the top, it knocked and cried, "Princess, youngest princess, open the door." She ran to see who it was, but when she opened the door, there sat the frog. She quickly slammed the door, came back, and sat down, but she was in a great fright. The king could see how her heart was beating, and said, "Why are you afraid, my child? Is there a giant at the door maybe, come to carry you away?" "Oh, no," she answered, "it's not a giant, only a nasty frog." "What does the frog want with you?" "Ah, dear Father, in the forest yesterday I was sitting by the well, playing, and my golden ball fell in the water. And because I was crying so hard, the frog went and fetched it up for me, and made me promise that he could be my best friend, but I never, never thought he'd get out of his water, and now he's here and wants to come inside with me." At that moment there was more knocking and a voice cried:

> "Princess, youngest princess,
>   open the door,
>   don't you know what you

172

said to me yesterday
by the cool well-water?
Princess, youngest princess,
open the door."

Then the king said, "If you made a promise, you must
keep it. Go, open the door for him." The princess went
and opened the door and the frog hopped in, following
her every footstep right up to her chair, and sat there
and cried, "Lift me up where you are." She hesitated
until finally the king commanded it. When the frog
was on her chair, he wanted to be up on the table, and
when he sat on the table he said, "Now push your
golden plate nearer, so we can eat together." She did,
but one could tell she did not like it. The frog ate
heartily, but as for her, every bite stuck in her throat.
Finally he said, "I have eaten till I am full, and now
I'm tired. Carry me to your room and make up your
silken bed so we can lie down and go to sleep." The
princess began to cry. She was afraid of the cold frog,
whom she could not bear to touch and who wanted to
sleep in her nice clean bed. But the king got angry and

173

said, "If someone helps you in your need, you must not look down on him afterwards." And so she took hold of the frog with two fingers, carried him upstairs, and set him in a corner, but when she was lying in bed he came crawling and said, "I'm tired too and want to sleep comfortably just like you. Lift me up, or I'll tell your father." Now this gets her really angry! She picked him up and she threw him against the wall as hard as she could: "Now will you be satisfied, you nasty frog!"

As he fell to the ground, however, he was no longer a frog but a prince with kind and beautiful eyes who, by her father's wishes, now became her friend and husband. And he told her how a wicked witch had put a spell on him and how nobody had been able to set him free from the well but she alone, and tomorrow they would go to his kingdom together. Then they went to sleep and next morning, when the sun woke them, a coach came driving up with eight white horses that had white ostrich feathers on their heads, all harnessed in golden chains, and in the back stood the young king's servant and it was his faithful Henry. Faithful Henry had been so grieved when his master was

changed into a frog that he had three iron bands laid around his heart to keep it from bursting with pain and sorrow. And the coach had come to fetch the young king home to his kingdom. Faithful Henry set them both inside and went and stood in the back and was overjoyed that his master had been freed. And when they had gone a little way, the prince heard a cracking behind him as if something had broken in two. He turned and cried:

"Henry, the carriage breaks apart."
"No, sire, it's not the carriage breaking,
  it's the iron band around my heart—
  my heart that lay so sorely aching
  while you were a frog, while you sat in the well."

Again, and once again, as they drove along, came the cracking sound, and each time the prince thought the coach was breaking apart but it was only another band bursting from around the heart of his faithful Henry because his master was free and happy.

The Poor Miller's Boy
and the Little Cat

In a mill lived an old miller who had neither wife nor children, and three young fellows worked for him. One day when they had been with him for some years, he said, "I am getting old; I want to sit behind the oven and take my ease. Go out into the world, and whichever one brings home the best horse shall have the mill and in return he must take care of me until I die." Now the third young boy was only an apprentice. The two others took him for a simpleton and begrudged him the mill, though as it turned out in the end he didn't even want it. So the three of them set out, and as they were leaving the village, the two said to simple John, "You might just as well stay here, *you'll* never get a horse as long as you live." But John went along anyway and at nightfall they came to a cave and went in and lay down to sleep. The two smart ones waited till John had fallen asleep, then they got up and made off and left Johnny lying there and thought they had done something very clever; oh, but it won't do you a bit of good! When the sun came up, John woke and there he lay deep in a cave. He peered all around and cried, "Dear God! Where am I!" and he rose and scrambled out of the cave and went into the forest and thought, Here I am, alone and forsaken. How shall I ever get a horse! And as he was walking along deep in thought he met a little speckled cat that spoke kindly to him and said, "Where are you off to, John?" "Oh, it's nothing you can help me with." "I know very well what it is you want," said the little cat. "You want a pretty horse. Come with me and be my faithful servant for seven years and I will give you one more handsome than anything you've seen in your whole life." What a strange cat, thought John, but I might as well go along and see if she is telling the truth. And so she took him with her to her bewitched little palace where she had nothing but cats to wait on her. They leaped nimbly up and down the stairs, happy and full of fun. In the evening, when they sat down to supper, there were three who made music; one played the double bass, another the violin, and the third put the trumpet to her mouth and blew up her cheeks for all she was worth. When they had eaten, the table was removed and the cat said, "Come, John, dance with me." "No," said he, "I don't dance with pussycats. That's something I have never done." "Then take him up to bed," she said to the little cats. So then one lighted him to his bedroom, one took off his shoes, one his stockings, and finally one blew out his candle. The next morning they came back and helped him out of bed; one put on his stockings, one tied his garters, one fetched his shoes, one washed him, and one dried his face with her tail. "That feels nice and soft," said John. John himself had to wait on the cat. Every day he had to chop firewood and had

a silver ax to do it with, and the wedges and the saw were all made of silver and the mallet was of copper. Well, and so he chopped and chopped and stayed in that house, had plenty of food and drink but never saw a soul except the speckled cat and her household. One day she said, "Go and mow the meadow and dry the hay," and she gave him a silver scythe and a golden whetstone and told him to be sure to bring everything back, and so John went and did as he was told and when he was finished he brought scythe, whetstone, and hay back home and said wasn't she going to give him his earnings. "No," said the cat, "first you must do one more thing. Here is silver lumber, and the carpenter's ax, the square, and everything you need all made of silver. Build me a little house with it." Well, and so John built the little house and when it was finished he said now he had done everything and still he didn't have a horse. And yet the seven years had passed as if they were six months. The cat asked him if he wouldn't like to see her horses. "Yes," said John, so she opened the little house and as she is opening up the door there are these twelve horses standing

183

there and oh, weren't they proud-looking, and didn't they shine and gleam like mirrors, it made his heart leap for joy. So then she gave him food and drink and said, "Go home. I won't give you your horse to take with you. In three days I will come and bring it after you." So then John got ready to leave and she showed him the way to the mill. But she hadn't even given him a new suit of clothes and he had to wear the old ragged smock he came in that had grown too short and tight for him in those seven years. Now when he got home, the two others were back as well, and though they had each brought a horse, the horse of one was blind and the other's horse was lame. They asked, "John, where's your horse?" "It's being sent after me in three days." They laughed and said, "Yes, John. Sure, John! Where would *you* get a horse? This is going to be something!" John came inside but the miller said they couldn't have him sitting at the table, he was so torn and ragged one would be ashamed if some-body dropped in, so they gave him a little bit of food to take outside; and in the evening, when they lay down to sleep, the two others would not let him in the bed, and he had to crawl into the goose pen and lie down on a little hard straw. And in the morning he wakes up and the three days have already passed and here comes a carriage drawn by six horses; my, it was a pleasure to see how they gleamed, and there's this servant and he's brought yet a seventh horse, which is for the poor miller's apprentice. But out of the carriage there stepped this magnificent princess and she came into the mill and the princess was the little speckled cat that poor John had served for seven years. She asked the miller where's the boy, the miller's apprentice? So then the miller says, "We couldn't have him in the mill he's so ragged, he's lying outside in the goose pen." So then the princess said they should go and get him at once. Well, so they went and got him out and he had to hold his little smock together to cover himself. And the servant unpacked magnificent clothes and washed him and dressed him, and when he was ready no king could have been more handsome. After that the lady asked to see the horses which the others had brought and one horse was blind and the other lame. So then she had the servant bring the seventh horse. When the miller saw it, he said that nothing like it had ever entered his yard. "Well, this is for the apprentice," said she. "Then he shall have the mill," said the miller, but the princess said he could have the horse and he could keep his mill and takes her faithful John and puts him in the carriage and drives off with him. And they drive to the little house he built with the silver tools and it is a great palace and everything in it is silver and gold and she marries him and he is rich—so rich he had plenty of everything as long as he lived. And that is why nobody should say that a simple person can never amount to anything.

Frederick and His Katelizabeth

There was a man called Frederick and a woman called Katelizabeth, and they got married and set up house together. One day Frederick said, "Katelizabeth, I'm going into the fields, and when I get back, you're to have a hot meal ready on the table for me and a cold drink to go with it." "Just you go along, Freddy dear," answered his Katelizabeth, "and you will see how nicely I will manage everything." Now when lunchtime drew near, she fetched a sausage out of the chimney, laid it in a frying pan, put in some butter,

187

and set it on the fire. The sausage began to cook and sizzle; Katelizabeth stood by and held the pan handle and thought thoughts, when it came to her: "While the sausage is cooking, why couldn't you be drawing the drink in the cellar?" And so she steadied the pan handle, fetched a jug, and went down into the cellar to draw beer. The beer ran into the jug; Katelizabeth watched it running, when it came to her: "Hey! The dog upstairs isn't chained and might steal the sausage out of the pan. That's all I need!" One, two, up the cellar steps, but the mutt already had the sausage in his mouth, trailing it behind him as he ran. Katelizabeth, no slouch, made after him and chased him a good way into the fields, but the dog was faster than Katelizabeth and never let go, and the sausage went skipping over the furrows. "Gone is gone," said Katelizabeth and she turned around and, because she was tired out from so much running, walked nice and slow, to cool off. All this time the beer was running out of the barrel because Katelizabeth had not turned the tap off, and when the jug was full and there was nowhere else for the beer to run, it ran all over the cellar floor and didn't stop until the whole barrel was empty. Katelizabeth saw the disaster from the steps. "Oh, hang," she said, "now what are you going to do so Frederick won't notice?" She thought awhile and in the end it came to her: they still had one sack of the beautiful wheat flour from the last church fair up in the loft; she could fetch it down and sprinkle it on the beer. "Yes indeed," said she. "Who saves in his day of plenty has in his day of need," and she climbed into the loft, carried down the sack, and threw it right on top of the full jug so that it overturned and Frederick's beer swam around the cellar too. "And quite right," said Katelizabeth. "Where one goes is where the rest should go as well," and she sprinkled the flour all over the cellar. When it was finished she was pleased with herself and said, "My, how neat and clean it looks!"

At lunchtime Frederick came home. "Well, wife, and what have you got for my lunch?" "Well, you see, Freddy," she answered, "I was going to fry you a sausage, but while I was drawing beer the dog stole it out of the pan, and while I was chasing the dog all the beer ran out, and when I wanted to soak up the beer with the wheat flour I knocked the jug over too, but don't you worry, the cellar is all nice and dry again." Said Frederick, "Katelizabeth, you shouldn't have done that! Let the dog steal the sausage and the beer run out of the barrel and pour out all our fine wheat flour too!" "Oh, but Freddy, I didn't know. You might have told me."

The man thought: "If that's the sort of wife you've got, you'll have to watch out." Now he had managed to save up a nice pile of thalers and he went and changed them into gold and said to Katelizabeth, "See these yellow chips? I'm going to put them in a pot and bury them in the cow shed, under the manger, but don't you go near them or there'll be trouble!" Said she, "Oh, all right, Freddy. I won't, I promise." Now when Frederick was gone, some peddlers came into the village selling earthern pots and pans and called at the young woman's house to ask if she would give them some business. "Ah, dear good people," said Katelizabeth, "I haven't got any money so I can't buy anything, but if you can use yellow chips, I could buy something." "Yellow chips—and why not? Let's have a look at them." "Go into the cow shed and dig under the manger, you'll find yellow chips; I'm not allowed to go near them." The rascals went and dug, found pure gold, and made off with it, leaving all their pots and pans standing around the house. Katelizabeth thought she ought to make some use of the new crockery, but as there was already plenty of everything in her kitchen she knocked the bottom out of every last pot and stuck them on the slats of the fence all the way around the house. When Frederick came home and saw the new decoration, he said, "Katelizabeth, what have you done!" "Bought them, Freddy dear, with the yellow chips from under the manger. But I never went near them myself. The peddlers had to dig it out for themselves." "Ah, wife," said Frederick, "now look what you've done! Those weren't chips but pure gold and it was our whole fortune. You shouldn't have done that." "But Freddy," answered she, "I didn't know. You should have told me."

Katelizabeth stood and thought awhile and then she said, "Listen, Freddy, we'll get the gold back all right. Let's run after those thieves." "Come on, then," said

Frederick, "we'll have a try. You bring along some butter and cheese so we'll have something to eat on the
way." "Oh, all right, Freddy, I certainly will." They
started on their way, and because Frederick was the
better walker, Katelizabeth came along behind. "Which
is all to the good," said she, "because when we turn
back I'll be that much farther ahead." Now she
came to a mountain where there were deep wagon ruts
on either side of the path. "Will you look at that,"
said Katelizabeth. "How they've worn down and torn
up and squashed this poor earth. It'll never heal as
long as it lives." And out of the goodness of her heart
she took the butter and smeared it on the ruts, right
and left, so the wheels would not hurt it anymore. And
as she stood bent over in her charitable act, one of the
cheeses rolled out of her pocket and down the mountain. Said Katelizabeth, "I've made my way up once
already, I'm not about to walk down again; let someone
else go and bring it back," so she took another cheese
and rolled it down the mountain, but the cheeses didn't
come back, so she sent a third one down, thinking:
"They're waiting for company, maybe they don't like

walking by themselves." But when all three of them stayed down there, she said, "I don't know what to make of it, and yet it could be the third one didn't find its way and got lost. I might as well send the fourth down to look for them." But the fourth did no better than the third and so Katelizabeth got cross and threw the fifth and sixth down too, and they were the last. For a while she stood and listened but they would not and would not come, so she said: "You'd be the right ones to send looking for death, you take such an everlasting time. You think I'm going to stand around here waiting for you? I'll go about my business and you can run after me, your legs are younger than mine." Katelizabeth walked off and found Frederick, who had stopped to wait because he felt like having something to eat. "All right, let's have what you brought with you." She handed him the dry bread. "Where is the butter and cheese?" asked the man. "Well, you see, Freddy," said Katelizabeth, "the butter I smeared on the wagon ruts and the cheeses will be here soon. One of them ran away, so I sent the others to go and bring it back." Said Frederick, "You shouldn't have done that, Katelizabeth, smear the butter all over the road and roll the cheeses down the mountain." "Well then, Freddy, you should have told me."

So together they ate the dry bread and Frederick said, "Katelizabeth, and did you lock up the house before you left?" "No, Freddy. You should have told me." "So run back home and take care of the door before we go any farther. And bring something else to eat. I'll wait here." Katelizabeth went home and thought, "Freddy wants something else to eat; he probably doesn't like butter and cheese, so I'll wrap some prunes in a cloth and take along a jug of vinegar to drink." Then she bolted the top part of the door, but the bottom half she lifted off the hinges and onto her shoulders, thinking that if she took care of the door, the house would be safe. Kateliza-beth took her time on the way, thinking: "All the more time for dear Frederick to rest up." When she got back to him she said, "Here you are, Freddy dear. Here's the front door so you can look after the house yourself." "Good heavens," said he, "what a clever wife! Takes the bottom door off the hinges, so anybody can run in, and bolts the top! It's too late now to go home again, but since you brought the door this far, you can carry it the rest of the way." "The door I'll carry, Freddy, but the prunes and the vinegar are getting too heavy: I'll hang them on the door. Let the door carry them."

Now they went into the forest looking for those rascals, but couldn't find them. Finally, when it was getting dark, they climbed into a tree where they meant to spend the night; but hardly had they got to the top and settled down when along came those fellows who carry away what doesn't come of its own accord and find things before they're lost, and sat down under the very tree in which Frederick and Katelizabeth were hiding, made themselves a fire, and got ready to divide up the loot. Frederick climbed down the other side, gathered stones, climbed back with them, and was going to stone the thieves to death. But the stones did not hit and the rascals said, "It will be morning soon; the wind is knocking the pine cones down." Katelizabeth was still carrying the door, and because its weight was pressing into her back, she thought it must be the prunes and said, "Dear Freddy, I've got to throw down the prunes." "No, Katelizabeth, not now," answered he, "the prunes might give us away." "Oh, but Freddy, I've got to, they're hurting me!" "Oh, all right, hang it, go ahead then." And so the prunes rolled down between the branches and the men below said, "It's bird droppings." A little while later, because the door was still pressing into her back, Katelizabeth said, "Dear Freddy, I've got to pour the vinegar out." "No, Katelizabeth, you mustn't do that, it might give us away." "Oh, but dear Freddy, I've just got to, it's hurting me so." "Oh, all right, hang it, go ahead then." And so she poured the vinegar out and it splattered the men below. They said to one another, "It's the dew already falling." Finally Katelizabeth thought, "Could it be the door digging into my back?" and said, "Freddy, I've got to throw the door down." "No, Katelizabeth, not now, it might give us away." "Oh, but Freddy, I've just got to, it's hurting too much!" "No, Katelizabeth, hold on tight!" "Oh dear, Freddy, I'm letting go." "Let it go then," answered Freddy angrily, "and the devil take it," and so the door fell down with such a clatter and the men below cried, "It's the devil coming down the tree," and bolted, leaving everything behind them. Early in

the morning, when the two climbed down, they found all their gold and carried it back home.

At home Frederick said, "Katelizabeth, now you must be a good girl and work hard." "Oh, I will, Freddy, I certainly will. I'll go out into the fields and mow the hay." Out in the fields Katelizabeth asked herself: "Shall I eat before I mow or shall I sleep before I mow? I know what, I'll eat first." And so Katelizabeth ate, and eating made her sleepy and she began to mow half in a dream and mowed her clothes in half, apron, skirt, and shirt. When Katelizabeth woke after a long sleep, there she was half naked and said to herself: "Is it me or isn't it? Aw, this is not me!" Meanwhile, night had come and so Katelizabeth ran into the village, knocked at her husband's window, and cried, "Freddy!" "What is it?" "I just wanted to see if Katelizabeth is in." "Sure," answered Frederick, "she's inside, lying down asleep." "Fine," said she, "then I must be home already," and walked away.

Outside, Katelizabeth met a couple of rogues and they wanted to go stealing. So Katelizabeth went to them and said, "I'll help you steal." The rascals thought she might know her way around the place and agreed. Katelizabeth went from house to house, crying, "Hey, everybody, what have you got for us to steal?" Thought the rascals, "This is going to be something," and wanted to get rid of Katelizabeth, so they said, "The pastor is growing turnips in a field outside the village, go pick us turnips." Katelizabeth went into the fields and began to pick but was so lazy she never straightened up, and a man who was passing saw her, stopped, and thought it was the devil rutting among the turnips, and ran to the pastor in the village and said, "Pastor, the devil's in your turnip field picking turnips." "Heavens!" answered the pastor, "and me with my lame foot; can't even get out there to exorcise him." Said the man, "I'll give you a piggyback," and carried him piggyback, and when they got out to the field Katelizabeth straightened up and stretched herself. "It's the devil!" cried the pastor and both ran away and the pastor in his great terror ran faster with his lame leg than the man who had carried him piggyback could run on his two healthy ones.

The Golden Bird

Once upon a time, in the old days, there was a king who had a beautiful garden behind his palace. In it there was a tree that bore golden apples. As the apples were getting ripe they were counted, but the very next morning one of them was missing. The king's sons told him about it, and he ordered that they should keep watch under the tree all night.

The king had three sons, the eldest of whom he sent into the garden as soon as it was night; but when midnight came he couldn't keep from going to sleep, and next morning another apple was missing. The next night the second son had to watch, but he had no better success; when midnight struck he fell asleep, and in the morning an apple was missing. Now it was the third son's time to watch, and he was all ready to, but the king didn't put much trust in him, and thought he'd be even less use than his brothers had been; at last, though, he let him go. The youth also lay down under the tree, watched, and didn't let himself go to sleep. As twelve struck, something rustled through the air, and in the moonlight he saw a bird flying along whose feathers were all shining with gold. The bird lit on the tree and had just pecked off an apple, when the youth shot an arrow at him. The bird flew away, but the arrow had struck his plumage, and one of his golden feathers fell down. The youth picked it up and next morning brought it to the king, and told him what had happened during the night. The king summoned his counselors, and every one of them declared that a feather like this was worth more than his whole kingdom put together. "If the feather is so precious," said the king, "just this one isn't enough for me. I must and will have the whole bird."

The oldest son set out, trusting to his own cleverness, and thought he'd as good as found the golden bird. When he'd gone some distance he saw a fox sitting on the edge of a wood, cocked his gun, and aimed at him. The fox said: "Don't shoot me, and in return I'll give you a piece of good advice. You're on the way to the golden bird, and this evening you'll come to a village where there're two inns right across from each other. One is all brightly lighted, and they're having a fine time inside. Don't go in, though, but go in the other, even if it looks bad."

"How can a foolish animal possibly give me reasonable advice?" thought the king's son, and pulled the trigger, but he missed the fox, who straightened out his tail and quickly ran off into the wood.

So then he set out on his way, and at evening came to the village where the two inns were. In one of them people were singing and dancing, the other had a wretched, dismal look. "I'd really be a fool," thought he, "if I went to that shabby inn and passed by the good one." So he went into the cheerful one, spent his time dancing and drinking, and forgot the bird, his father, and all good teachings.

When some time had gone by and the eldest son still hadn't come home, the second set out on his way to look for the golden bird. The fox met him just as he'd met the eldest, and gave him the same good advice that he paid no attention to. He came to the two inns; his brother was standing at the window of the one, from which the sound of merrymaking came, and called to him. He couldn't resist, went inside, and from then on lived only for pleasure.

Again some time went by, and then the king's youngest son wanted to set out and try his luck, but his father wouldn't allow it. "It's no use," said he. "He has even less chance than his brothers to find the golden bird, and if he meets with some misfortune he won't know what to do. He's not much, at best." But finally, since the youth gave him no peace, he let him go.

Again the fox was sitting on the edge of the wood, begged for his life, and gave his good advice. The youth was good-natured and said: "Don't worry, little fox. I won't hurt you."

"You won't regret it," answered the fox, "and to get along a little faster, climb onto my tail." And hardly had he sat down than the fox began to run, and away they went over hill and dale so that his hair whistled in the wind. When they came to the village, the youth got off, followed the good advice, and without even looking around went into the small inn, where he quietly spent the night. Next morning, as soon as he got out into the fields, there sat the fox already, and said: "I'll tell you what else you've got to do. Keep going straight ahead and finally you'll come to a castle in front of which a whole troop of soldiers will be lying. But don't you worry about them because they'll be snoring away, fast asleep. Walk through them and go straight into the castle, and go through all the rooms. Last of all you'll come to a chamber in which there's a wooden cage hanging, and in it a golden bird. Beside it is an empty gold cage, just for show, but be sure that you don't take the bird out of the plain cage and put it in the grand one, or you'll be in a mighty bad fix." After these words the fox straightened out his tail again, and the king's son got on; then away they went over hill and dale so that his hair whistled in the wind.

When he got to the castle, he found everything just as the fox had said. The king's son went into the chamber in which the golden bird sat in the wooden cage, with the golden one beside it. Three golden apples were lying in the room, too. Then he thought that it would be ridiculous to leave the beautiful bird in such an ugly, ordinary cage; he opened the door, seized it, and put it in the golden one. But that very instant the bird gave a piercing cry. The soldiers woke, rushed in, and led him off to prison. The next morning he was brought before a court and, since he confessed everything, sentenced to death. But the king said that he would spare him his life on one condition, that he bring him the golden horse that could run swifter than the wind, and then he'd give him the golden bird besides.

The king's son set out on his way, but he sighed and felt very sad, for how was he to find the golden horse? Then all at once he saw sitting by the road his old friend, the fox. "You see what's happened because you didn't listen to me," said the fox. "Cheer up, though, I'll look out for you and tell you how to get to the golden horse. You must go straight ahead, and that way you'll come to a castle in which the horse is standing in a stable. The grooms will be lying in front of the stable, but they'll be snoring away fast asleep, and you can easily lead out the golden horse. But one thing you've got to watch out for: put the plain wood and leather saddle on him, not the golden one hanging by it, or you'll be in a mighty bad fix." Then the fox straightened out his tail, the king's son got on, and away they went over hill and dale so that the wind whistled in his hair.

Everything happened just as the fox said it would. He went into the stable where the golden horse was standing, but when he was about to put the plain saddle on the horse, he thought: "It will spoil the looks of such a beautiful animal if I don't put on the good saddle it's entitled to." But hardly had the golden saddle touched it than the horse began to whinny loudly. The grooms woke up, seized the youth, and threw him in prison. The next morning he was sentenced to death by the court, but the king promised to grant him his life and the golden horse besides, if he could bring back the beautiful princess from the golden castle.

With a heavy heart the youth set out on his way, but soon, to his joy, he met the faithful fox. "I should just leave you to your bad luck," said the fox, "but I'm sorry for you and will help you out of your difficulty one more time. This road leads straight to the golden castle. You'll get there this evening, and tonight when every-thing is still, then the beautiful princess will go to the bathhouse to bathe. And when she goes in, leap out at her and give her a kiss. Then she'll follow you, and you can take her away with you. Only don't let her say goodbye to her parents, or you'll be in a mighty bad fix." Then the fox straightened out his tail, the king's son got on, and away they went over hill and dale so that the wind whistled in his hair.

When he got to the golden castle, it was just as the fox had said. He waited until midnight; when everyone lay in deep sleep and the beautiful maiden went to the bathhouse, he sprang out and gave her a kiss. She said that she'd gladly go with him, but implored him, with tears in her eyes, to let her say goodbye to her parents. At first he resisted her prayers, but when she wept and

wept and threw herself at his feet, he at last gave in. But hardly had the maiden got to her father's bedside than the youth was seized and put in prison.

Next morning the king said to him: "Your life is forfeit, and you'll be pardoned only if you move the mountain that stands in front of my window, that I can't see over, and you must manage it within eight days. If you succeed you shall have my daughter as your reward." The king's son started to dig and shovel without stopping, but when after seven days he saw how little he had accomplished and how all his work was as good as nothing, he became completely wretched and gave up all hope. But on the evening of the seventh day the fox appeared and said: "You don't deserve my looking out for you, but just walk over there and go to sleep. I'll do the work for you."

The next morning, when he woke up and looked out the window, the mountain had disappeared. Full of joy, the youth hurried to the king and told him that his condition had been satisfied, and that the king, whether he wanted to or not, must keep his word and give him his daughter.

So they set out together, and it wasn't long before the faithful fox came up to them. "You've certainly got the best thing, but the golden horse goes along with the maiden from the golden castle, too."

"How shall I get it?" asked the youth.

"That I'll tell you," answered the fox. "First bring the beautiful maiden to the king who sent you to the golden castle. Then they'll be overjoyed, they'll gladly give you the golden horse, and will lead it out to you. Get on it right away, offer your hand to all of them as you tell them goodbye, seize the beautiful maiden, and when you've got hold of her, swing her up and gallop away; and nobody will be able to catch you, for your horse is swifter than the wind."

Everything was accomplished successfully, and the king's son carried off the beautiful princess on the golden horse. The fox didn't stay behind, but said to the youth: "Now I'll help you get the golden bird too. When you're near the castle where the bird is, let the maiden dismount, and I'll take charge of her. Then ride the golden horse into the courtyard of the castle. They'll be overjoyed to see it, and will bring you out the golden bird. As soon as you've got the cage in your hand, gallop back to us and take the maiden away with you again."

When the plan had succeeded and the king's son was about to ride home with his treasures, the fox said: "Now you must reward me for my help."

"What do you want for it?" asked the youth.

"When we get to that wood over there, shoot me dead and chop off my head and feet."

"That would be a fine way to show my gratitude," said the king's son. "I couldn't possibly do that for you."

Said the fox: "If you won't do it, then I must leave you. But before I go I'll give you a piece of good advice. Watch out for two things: don't buy any gallows flesh and don't sit on the edge of any well." With that he ran off into the wood.

The youth thought: "That's a queer beast with some crazy ideas. Who would ever buy gallows flesh? And never have I had the slightest desire to sit down on the edge of a well."

He rode on with the beautiful maiden, and his road carried him back through the village where his two brothers had stayed. There was a great uproar and commotion, and when he asked what was wrong, they said that two men were about to be hanged. When he got nearer he saw that it was his brothers, who had done all kinds of wicked things and had wasted everything they owned. He asked whether they couldn't be set free. "If you'll pay for them," answered the people, "but why waste your money on these wicked men and buy them off?" But he didn't even hesitate, paid for them, and when they'd been freed, all of them went on their way together.

They came to the wood where the fox had met them first, and it was cool and pleasant inside and the sun burning hot, so the two brothers said: "Let's rest awhile here on the edge of this well and have something to eat and drink." He agreed, and while they were talking he forgot himself and sat down on the edge of the well, not suspecting any harm. But the two brothers pushed him over backwards into the well, took the maiden, the horse, and the bird, and rode home to their father. "Here we've brought you not just the golden bird, we've carried off the golden horse and the girl from the golden castle besides." The people were overjoyed, but the

214

horse didn't eat, the bird didn't sing, and the maiden sat and wept.

The youngest brother hadn't perished, though. By good luck the well was dry, and he fell on some soft moss without being hurt, but wasn't able to get out again. Even in this extremity the faithful fox didn't forsake him. He came and jumped down to him, and scolded him for having forgotten his advice. "Still, though, I can't help it," said he. "I'll bring you back to the light of day." He told him to grasp his tail and hold on tight, and then he pulled him up.

"You're still not out of danger," said the fox. "Your brothers weren't sure you were dead, and have put guards around the forest who'll kill you if you let them see you." There by the road sat a poor man, and the youth changed clothes with him and in this way got to the king's palace. Nobody recognized him, but the bird began to sing, the horse began to eat, and the maiden stopped weeping. Astonished, the king asked: "What does this mean?"

Then the maiden said: "I don't know, but I was so sad, and now I'm so happy. I feel as if my true bridegroom had come." She told him everything that had happened, though the other brothers had threatened to kill her if she betrayed anything. The king ordered all the people in his palace to be brought before him; so the youth, looking like a poor beggar in his rags, came too. The maiden, though, recognized him immediately and threw her arms around his neck. The wicked brothers were seized and put to death, while he was married to the beautiful maiden and made the king's heir.

But what became of the poor fox? A long time afterward the king's son once again was walking in the wood, when the fox met him and said: "Now you have everything you can wish for, but my misery goes on without an end, and yet you have it in your power to free me." And once more he begged him to shoot him and chop off his head and feet. So he did, and no sooner was it done than the fox turned into a man, and was none other than the brother of the beautiful princess, freed at last from the spell under which he had lain. And now there was nothing lacking to their happiness, so long as they all lived.

Bearskin

Once upon a time there was a young fellow who enlisted in the army, carried himself bravely, and was always out in front where it rained bullets. As long as there was a war on, everything went well, but when they made peace he was discharged and the captain said he could go where he pleased. His parents had died, and he had no place to call home, so he went to his brothers and asked them to take care of him until a new war started. But the brothers were hardhearted men and said, "What are we to do with you! You are no good to us. Go make your own way as best you can." The soldier had nothing except his gun, which he took on his shoulder, and so he went out into the world. He came to a great heath on which there was nothing except a circle of trees. He sat down sadly and mused about his fate. I have no money, he thought, I have learned no trade except how to make war, and now they have made peace and don't need me any more. I can see that I must starve to death. All of a sudden he heard a great rustling and rushing, and when he looked around, there stood a stranger in a green coat, a fine-looking man but with a nasty horse's hoof. "I know what troubles you," the man said. "You shall have such an abundance of the world's goods that however hard you try, you'll never use it up, but first I have to make sure that you are not afraid. I don't want to waste my money." "A soldier and fear, they don't go together!" he answered. "Put me to the test." "Very well, then," said the man, "look behind you." The soldier turned around and saw a big bear trotting toward him and growling. "Oho," cried the soldier, "I'm going to tickle your nose for you so you won't feel like growling any more," took aim, and shot the bear in the muzzle so that it fell in a heap and never stirred again. "I can see," said the stranger, "you don't lack courage, but there is one other condition you must fulfill." "So long as it does not threaten my eternal soul," answered the soldier, who knew very well who it was standing before him, "I'm ready for anything." "Judge for yourself," answered Greencoat. "For the next seven years, you may neither wash yourself nor comb your beard or hair nor cut your nails nor pray the Our Father. And I will give you a jacket and an overcoat which you must wear all the time. If you die within the seven years you're mine, if you stay alive you are free and rich for the rest of your days." The soldier thought of his great need and how often he had faced death in the past, and was ready to dare it again, and so he agreed. The devil took off his green jacket and gave it to the soldier and said, "When you wear this coat and reach into your pocket, you will always find your hand full of money." Then he skinned the pelt off the bear and said, "This shall be your overcoat and your bed, because you must sleep in it, nor may you lie down on any other bed. And because of this costume you shall be called Bearskin." With that the devil disappeared.

The soldier put the coat on, reached into the pocket, and found the devil as good as his word. Then he hung the bearskin around his shoulders and went out into the world, was in good spirits, and left nothing undone that was good for him and bad for his money. In the first year things were still bearable. By the second year he began to look like a monster. His hair almost covered his face, his beard looked like a piece of coarse cloth, his fingers had grown claws, and his face was so dirty, if you had sowed cress on it, it would have sprouted. People ran away when they saw him, but he always gave money to the poor so they would pray for him not to die within the seven years. Because he paid well he always found a roof for his head wherever he went.

Now in the fourth year he came to an inn and the innkeeper refused to take him and would not even give him a place in the stable because he was afraid he might frighten the horses, but when Bearskin reached into his pocket and brought out a handful of ducats the innkeeper's heart softened. He let him have a room in the back, but he had to promise not to let anybody see him so as not to give the house a bad name.

In the evening Bearskin was sitting alone, wishing with all his heart that the seven years were past, when he heard loud wailing in the next room. He had a kind heart and opened the door and saw an old man crying with all his might, beating his hands together over his head. Bearskin came closer. The man jumped up and would have fled, but when he heard a human voice he let himself be calmed. Bearskin urged him so kindly, he even got him to disclose the cause of his misery. His fortune had dwindled a little at a time until he and his daughters were starving, and so poor was he that he could not even pay the innkeeper, who threatened to put him in jail. "If that's all that troubles you," said Bearskin, "I have plenty of money." He called the innkeeper, paid him off, and even put a purse of gold into the wretched man's pocket.

When the old man saw himself relieved of his worries he did not know how to show his gratitude. "Come

with me," said he. "My daughters are marvels of
beauty, choose one of them for your wife. When she
hears what you have done for me, she will not refuse.
You do look a little strange but she'll soon put you to
rights." Bearskin liked the idea very well and went
with him. When the oldest daughter caught sight of his
face, it gave her such a fright she ran away screaming.
The second one stayed and looked him over from head
to foot but she said, "How can I take a husband who
doesn't look human? I prefer the shaved bear who was
on show here once, and pretended to be a man. At least
he wore a fur coat like a hussar and had white gloves.
If this one were merely ugly, I could get used to it."
But the youngest said, "Dear Father, he must be a good
man, who helped you in your need. If, in return, you
promised him a bride, your word must be kept." It was
a pity that Bearskin's face was covered with dirt and
hair or one might have seen how his heart leaped for
joy. He took a ring from his finger, broke it in two, gave
her one half and kept the other himself. In her half he
wrote his name and in his half he wrote her name and
asked her to keep her piece safe. Then he took his leave

and said, "I have to travel another three years. If I come back we will celebrate our wedding, but if I don't return, you are free, because that means I am dead. But pray God to keep me alive."

The poor bride dressed herself all in black, and whenever she thought about her bridegroom, tears came into her eyes. From her sisters she had nothing but mockery and gibes. "Take care," said the eldest, "when you give him your hand, he will slap it with his paw." "Look out," said the second, "bears love sweets, and if he likes you he will gobble you up." "You must do everything he wants," the oldest started in again, "or he'll begin to growl," and the second one added, "But the wedding will be fun. Bears are good dancers." The bride said nothing and would not let them change her heart. But Bearskin roamed through the world from one place to another, did good deeds wherever he could, and gave generously to the poor so they would pray for him. Finally, when the last day of the seven years had dawned, he went back onto the heath and sat down under the circle of trees. Soon there was a great rustling and rushing, and the devil stood before him and looked at him crossly, threw him his old jacket, and asked for his green one back. "Not so fast," answered Bearskin, "first you have to clean me up." Willy-nilly, the devil had to fetch water and wash Bearskin and comb his hair and cut his nails, and soon he looked like a brave warrior again and much handsomer than before.

When, happily, the devil had taken himself off, Bearskin felt gay at heart. He went into town, put on a splendid velvet coat, got into a carriage drawn by four white horses, and drove to the house of his bride. Nobody knew him. The father took him for a high-ranking officer, brought him into the room where his daughters were sitting, and made him sit between the two eldest; they poured him wine, helped him to the choicest morsels, and thought they had never seen such a handsome man. But the bride sat across from him in her black dress, did not raise her eyes, and never said a word. Finally, when he asked the father to give him one of his daughters for a wife, the two eldest jumped up and ran into their room to put on their most splendid gowns because each imagined she was the chosen one. When the stranger was alone with his bride, he took

out his half of the ring, dropped it into a beaker of wine, and handed it across the table to her. She accepted, and when she had drunk it and found the half ring at the bottom, her heart began to beat. She took out the other half, which she wore on a ribbon around her neck, held the two pieces together and they matched perfectly, and he said, "I am your promised bridegroom whom you saw as Bearskin, but by God's grace I have my human form and am clean again." He came to her, embraced her, and gave her a kiss. At that moment the two sisters returned all dressed up, and when they saw that the handsome man belonged to their youngest sister and heard that it was Bearskin, they ran out of the room full of rage and fury. One drowned herself in the well, the other hanged herself on a tree. In the evening someone knocked at the door, and when the bridegroom opened it, it was the devil in his green coat, who said, "You see, now I've got two souls, instead of your one."

Godfather Death

A poor man had twelve children and worked night and day just to get enough bread for them to eat. Now when the thirteenth came into the world, he did not know what to do and in his misery ran out onto the great highway to ask the first person he met to be godfather. The first to come along was God, and he already knew what it was that weighed on the man's mind and said, "Poor man, I pity you. I will hold your child at the font and I will look after it and make it happy upon earth." "Who are you?" asked the man. "I am God."

"Then I don't want you for a godfather," the man said. "You give to the rich and let the poor go hungry." That was how the man talked because he did not understand how wisely God shares out wealth and poverty, and thus he turned from the Lord and walked on. Next came the Devil and said, "What is it you want? If you let me be godfather to your child, I will give him gold as much as he can use, and all the pleasures of the world besides." "Who are you?" asked the man. "I am the Devil." "Then I don't want you for a godfather," said the man. "You deceive and mislead mankind." He walked on and along came spindle-legged Death striding toward him and said, "Take me as godfather." The man asked, "Who are you?" "I am Death who makes all men equal." Said the man, "Then you're the one for me; you take rich and poor without distinction. You shall be godfather." Answered Death, "I will make your child rich and famous, because the one who has me for a friend shall want for nothing." The man said, "Next Sunday is the baptism. Be there in good time." Death appeared as he had promised and made a perfectly fine godfather.

When the boy was of age, the godfather walked in one

day, told him to come along, and led him out into the woods. He showed him an herb which grew there and said, "This is your christening gift. I shall make you into a famous doctor. When you are called to a patient's bedside I will appear and if I stand at the sick man's head you can boldly say that you will cure him and if you give him some of this herb he will recover. But if I stand at the sick man's feet, then he is mine, and you must say there is no help for him and no doctor on this earth could save him. But take care not to use the herb against my will or it could be the worse for you."

It wasn't long before the young man had become the most famous doctor in the whole world. "He looks at a patient and right away he knows how things stand, whether he will get better or if he's going to die." That is what they said about him, and from near and far the people came, took him to see the sick, and gave him so much money he became a rich man. Now it happened that the king fell ill. The doctor was summoned to say if he was going to get well. When he came to the bed, there stood Death at the feet of the sick man, so that no herb on earth could have done him any good. If I could only just this once outwit Death! thought the doctor. He'll be annoyed, I know, but I am his godchild and he's sure to turn a blind eye. I'll take my chance. And so he lifted the sick man and laid him the other way around so that Death was standing at his head. Then he gave him some of the herb and the king began to feel better and was soon in perfect health. But Death came toward the doctor, his face dark and angry, threatened him with raised forefinger, and said, "You have tricked me. This time I will let it pass because you are my godchild, but if you ever dare do such a thing again, you put your own head in the noose and it is you I shall carry away with me."

Soon after that, the king's daughter lapsed into a deep illness. She was his only child, he wept day and night until his eyes failed him and he let it be known that whoever saved the princess from death should become her husband and inherit the crown. When the doctor came to the sick girl's bed, he saw Death at her feet. He ought to have remembered his godfather's warning, but the great beauty of the princess and the happiness of becoming her husband so bedazzled him that he threw caution to the winds, nor did he see Death's angry glances and how he lifted his hand in the air and threatened him with his bony fist. He picked the sick girl up and laid her head where her feet had lain, then he gave her some of the herb and at once her cheeks reddened and life stirred anew.

When Death saw himself cheated of his property the second time, he strode toward the doctor on his long legs and said, "It is all up with you, and now it is your turn," grasped him harshly with his ice-cold hand so that the doctor could not resist, and led him to an underground cave, and here he saw thousands upon thousands of lights burning in rows without end, some big, some middle-sized, others small. Every moment some went out and others lit up so that the little flames seemed to be jumping here and there in perpetual exchange. "Look," said Death, "these are the life lights of mankind. The big ones belong to children, the middle-sized ones to married couples in their best years, the little ones belong to very old people. Yet children and the young often have only little lights." "Show me my life light," said the doctor, imagining that it must be one of

the big ones. Death pointed to a little stub threatening to go out and said, "Here it is." "Ah, dear godfather," said the terrified doctor, "light me a new one, do it, for my sake, so that I may enjoy my life and become king and marry the beautiful princess." "I cannot," answered Death. "A light must go out before a new one lights up." "Then set the old on top of a new one so it can go on burning when the first is finished," begged the doctor. Death made as if to grant his wish, reached for a tall new taper, but because he wanted revenge he purposely fumbled and the little stub fell over and went out. Thereupon the doctor sank to the ground and had himself fallen into the hands of death.

Many-Fur

Once upon a time there was a king and he had a wife who was the most beautiful woman in the world and had hair of pure gold and the two had a daughter as beautiful as her mother and her hair was just as golden. It happened that the queen became ill, and when she felt that she was about to die, she called the king and asked him to promise her that after she was dead he would marry no woman who was not as beautiful as she and had not the same golden hair, and when the king had promised, she died.

For a long time the king was so sad he never thought of a second wife, but finally his counselors urged him to remarry. And so messengers were sent to all the princesses but none was as beautiful as the queen who was dead and of course there was no one in the whole wide world who had such golden hair. One day the king's eye happened to fall on his daughter and he saw that she looked exactly like her mother and had the same golden hair and he thought, You'll never find anyone in all the world more beautiful than that, you have to marry your daughter, and at the same moment felt so great a love for her that he at once proclaimed his wishes to his counselors and to the princess. The counselors tried to talk him out of it, but in vain. The princess was horrified at her father's wicked plan but she was a clever girl and told the king that he must first get her three dresses, one as golden as the sun, one as white as the moon, and one that glittered like the stars; also a coat made of a thousand different kinds of fur, and every animal in the kingdom would have to give up a piece of its hide for it. But the king's desire was so fierce that he put his whole kingdom to work.

His huntsmen had to trap every animal and skin it and the hides were made into a coat, and so it wasn't long before he brought the princess what she had wished and she said she would marry him the next day. But in the night she gathered up the presents from her betrothed —a gold ring, a little golden spinning wheel, and a little golden reel—and put the three dresses of sun, moon, and stars into a walnut shell; then she blackened her face and hands with soot, put on her coat of many furs, and ran away. All night she walked until she came to a great forest where she would be safe, and because she was tired she sat down in a hollow tree and fell asleep.

It was already broad day and still she slept. It happened that the king to whom she was betrothed was hunting nearby and his dogs came and ran around the tree and sniffed at it. The king sent his huntsmen to see what kind of animal might be hiding in the tree and they came back and said it was the most peculiar animal they had ever seen in all their lives. Its skin was made of many furs and it was lying there fast asleep. And so the king gave orders for the animal to

238

be caught and tied on the back of the wagon. But as the huntsmen were pulling it out they saw it was a girl and they tied her onto the back of the wagon and took her home with them. "Many-Fur," they said, "you'll do for the kitchen. You can carry wood and water and sweep up the ashes." And they gave her a little stall under the stair, where no daylight ever came: "Here's where you can live and sleep." And so now she had to work in the kitchen and helped the cook, plucked the chickens, raked the fire, cleaned the vegetables, and did all the dirty work. She worked so neatly, the cook was pleased with her and some evenings he called Many-Fur and gave her some of the leftovers to eat. But before the king went to bed she had to go upstairs to take off his boots and always when she had taken off one of them the king would throw it at her head.

In this way Many-Fur lived a long time, wretchedly enough. Ah, lovely princess, what is to become of you? Once there was a ball in the palace. Many-Fur thought, Here's a chance to get a glimpse of my dear sweetheart, and went to the cook and asked him if he wouldn't let her go upstairs for a while and stand at the door and

look in on all the splendor. "Go along then," he said,
"but don't stay away for more than half an hour, you
still have all the ashes to sweep up tonight." And so
Many-Fur took her oil lamp and went to her little stall,
and washed the soot off her face and hands so that her
beauty blossomed forth like a flower in the new spring;
then she took off her coat of fur, opened the walnut, and
took out the dress that shone like the sun. And when
she was all dressed she went in and everybody made
way for her because they thought it must be some ele-
gant princess coming into the hall. The king at once
took her hand for the dance and as they were dancing
he thought, How this beautiful, strange princess resem-
bles my dear bride, and the longer he looked at her the
more she seemed to resemble her, so that he was almost
sure. He was going to ask her when the dance was
over, but as soon as she had finished she bowed and
was gone before the king so much as knew what had
happened. He sent to question the watchmen, but nobody had seen the princess leave the palace. Meanwhile, she had run to her little stall, quickly taken off
her dress, blackened her face and hands, and put her

coat of fur back on. Then she went into the kitchen and began sweeping the ashes, but the cook said, "Let that go till tomorrow. I want to go up too and watch the dancing for a bit, and you can cook the king's soup, but take care not to let a hair fall in the pot or I'll never give you anything to eat again." So Many-Fur cooked the king a bread soup and when it was done she put in the gold ring which he had given her. Now when the ball was over, the king asked for his bread soup and it tasted so good he thought he had never eaten a better one, and when he had finished and found the golden ring lying at the bottom, he looked at it closely and saw it was his wedding ring and he was astonished and could not understand how it had got there. He summoned the cook. The cook got angry with Many-Fur and said, "If you have let a hair fall in the soup, I'm going to beat you." But when the cook came upstairs, the king asked him who had cooked the soup because it was better than usual, and so he had to confess that Many-Fur had made it and the king told him to send her up.

When Many-Fur came before the king he said, "Who

are you and what are you doing in my palace? Where did you get the ring that was in my soup?" She answered, "I'm only a poor child who has lost her father and her mother. I have nothing and am good for nothing except to have boots thrown at my head, and I don't know anything about the ring either," and she ran away.

After that there was another ball and again Many-Fur asked the cook to let her go upstairs. The cook let her go but only for half an hour and then she was to come back and cook the king his bread soup. Many-Fur went to her little stall, washed herself clean, and took out the moon dress, more pure and shining than the new-fallen snow, and when she came upstairs the dance was just beginning and the king gave her his hand and danced with her and was no longer in any doubt that it was his bride because no one else, in all the world, had such golden hair; but when the dance was over the princess was gone and every effort was in vain, the king could not find her and had not been able to say one word to her. Meanwhile she had changed back into Many-Fur with her black face and hands and stood in the kitchen cooking the king's bread soup, and the cook had gone upstairs to watch the dancing. And when the soup was finished she put in the little golden spinning wheel. The king ate the soup and it seemed to him it tasted even better, and when he found the golden spinning wheel at the bottom he was even more astonished because it was the one he had given to his bride. The cook was sent for, and then Many-Fur, but again she would say only that she knew nothing and was only good to have boots thrown at her head.

And for the third time the king held a ball and hoped his bride would come again and was sure he could hold on to her. And again Many-Fur asked the cook if he wouldn't let her go upstairs. He scolded her and said, "You are a witch and put something in the soup; you can cook better than I." But she begged so hard and promised to do everything right, so he let her go upstairs for half an hour, and she put on the dress that glittered like the stars at night and went upstairs and danced with the king. It seemed to him that he had never seen her as beautiful as this. While they were dancing he slipped a ring on her finger and he had ordered the dance to last a long, long time. But still he could not hold her or say a word to her, for when the dance was over she disappeared into the crowd before he had time to turn around. She got to her little stall and because it had been more than half an hour she quickly undressed, but in her hurry she could not blacken herself all over and left one finger white, and when she came to the kitchen the cook was already gone and so she quickly cooked the bread soup and put in the golden reel. The king found it as he had the ring and the spinning wheel and now he was sure that his bride was near because only she alone could have had these presents. Many-Fur was summoned and again she meant to talk her way out of it and make off, but as she was running away, the king saw the white finger and caught hold of her hand and he found the ring he had slipped onto it and tore off her coat and the golden hair came flowing out and it was his dearest bride and the cook was richly rewarded and they celebrated their wedding and lived happily until they died.

Rapunzel

Once upon a time there was a man and wife who had long wished for a child. Finally the woman was filled with hope and expected God would grant her wish. The couple had a little window in back of their house and you could look down into a magnificent garden full of the loveliest flowers and herbs. But the garden was surrounded by a high wall and nobody dared go in because it belonged to a great and powerful witch who was feared by all the world. One day the woman was standing by the window looking into the garden and saw a bed planted with the most beautiful lettuce, of the kind they call Rapunzel. It looked so fresh and green that she began to crave it and longed fiercely to taste the lettuce. Each day her longing grew and because she knew she could not have it, she began to pine and look pale and miserable. Her husband got frightened and said, "Dear wife, are you ill?" "Ah," said she, "if I cannot have some lettuce from the garden behind our house, I will die." The husband loved her very much, and said to himself, You can't let your wife die; fetch her some lettuce, whatever the cost may be. In the evening, therefore, at twilight, he clambered over the wall into the witch's garden, hurriedly dug up a handful of lettuce, and brought it home to his wife, and she made herself a salad right away and ate it ravenously. It tasted good, oh so good that the next day she craved it three times as much. If she was to have any peace, her husband must climb into the garden once again. And so at twilight he went back, but when he got down the other side of the wall he stood horrified, for there, standing right in front of him, was the witch. "How dare you come climbing into my garden, stealing my lettuce like a thief?" said she, and her eyes were angry. "You shall pay for this!" "Ah, no, please," cried the man. "Let justice be tempered with mercy! Only my despair made me do what I did. My wife saw your lettuce out of our window and felt such a craving that she had to have some, or die." And so the witch's anger began to cool and she said, "If that is so, I will allow you to take as much lettuce as you want on one condition: You must give me the child your wife brings into the world. It shall be well cared for. I will look after it like a mother." In his terror the man agreed to everything and no sooner had the wife been brought to bed than the witch appeared. She named the child Rapunzel and took it away with her.

Rapunzel grew into the most beautiful child under the sun. When she was twelve years old, the witch locked her up in a tower that stood in the forest and had neither stair nor door, only way at the top there was a little window. If the witch wanted to get inside, she came and stood at the bottom and called:

"Rapunzel, Rapunzel,
Let down your hair."

Rapunzel had magnificent long hair, fine as spun gold. Now when she heard the voice of the witch, she unfastened her braids, wound them around a hook on the window, and let the hair fall twenty feet to the ground below, and the witch climbed up.

After some years it happened that the king's son rode through the forest, past the tower, and heard singing so lovely he stood still and listened. It was Rapunzel in her loneliness, who made the time pass by letting her sweet voice ring through the forest. The prince wanted to climb up the tower and looked for the door but could not find one. So he rode home, but the singing had so moved his heart he came back to the forest day after day and listened. Once, when he was standing there behind a tree, he saw how a witch came along and heard her calling:

"Rapunzel, Rapunzel,
Let down your hair."

And then Rapunzel let her braids down and the witch climbed up. "If that's the ladder one takes to the top, I'll try my luck too." Next day, when it began to get dark, he went to the tower and called:

> "Rapunzel, Rapunzel,
> Let down your hair."

And the hair was let down and the prince climbed up.

At first Rapunzel was very much frightened when a man stepped in, because her eyes had never seen anything like him before, but the prince spoke very kindly to her and told her how his heart had been so moved by her singing he had wanted to see her. And so Rapunzel lost her fear, and when he asked her if she would take him for her husband and she saw how young and beautiful he was, she thought, He will love me better than my old godmother, and said, "Yes," and put her hand in his hand. She said, "I would like to go with you but I don't know how to get down from here. Every time you come, bring a skein of silk with you. I will braid a ladder and when the ladder is finished I will climb down and you will take me on your horse." Until that time the prince was to come to her every evening, for by day came the old woman. The witch knew nothing about all this until one day Rapunzel opened her mouth and said, "Tell me, Godmother, why is it you are so much harder to pull up than the young prince? He's with me in the twinkling of an eye." "Oh, wicked child!" cried the witch. "What is this! I thought I had kept you from all the world and still you deceive me," and in her fury she grasped Rapunzel's lovely hair, wound it a number of times around her left hand, and with her right hand seized a pair of scissors and snip snap, the beautiful braids lay on the floor. And so pitiless was she that she took poor Rapunzel into a wilderness and left her there to live in great misery and need.

On the evening of the day on which she had banished Rapunzel, the witch tied the severed braids to the hook at the window, and when the prince came and called:

> "Rapunzel, Rapunzel,
> Let down your hair,"

she let the hair down. The prince climbed up and found not his dearest Rapunzel but the witch looking at him

with her wicked, venomous eyes. "Ah, ha," cried she mockingly, "you come to fetch your ladylove, but the pretty bird has flown the nest and stopped singing. The cat's got it and will scratch out your eyes too. You have lost Rapunzel and will never see her again." The prince was beside himself with grief and in his despair jumped out of the tower. His life was saved but he had fallen into thorns that pierced his eyes. And so he stumbled blindly about the forest, living on roots and berries, and did nothing but wail and weep for the loss of his dearest wife. And so for years he wandered in misery; finally he came into the wilderness where Rapunzel lived meagerly with her twin children, a boy and a girl, whom she had brought into the world. He heard her voice and it sounded so familiar to him. He walked toward it and Rapunzel recognized him and fell around his neck and cried. Two of her tears moistened his eyes and they regained their light and he could see as well as ever. He took her to his kingdom, where he was received with joy, and they lived happily and cheerfully for many years to come.

Snow-White and the Seven Dwarfs

Once it was the middle of winter, and the snowflakes fell from the sky like feathers. At a window with a frame of ebony a queen sat and sewed. And as she sewed and looked out at the snow, she pricked her finger with the needle, and three drops of blood fell in the snow. And in the white snow the red looked so beautiful that she thought to herself: "If only I had a child as white as snow, as red as blood, and as black as the wood in the window frame!" And after a while she had a little daughter as white as snow, as red as blood, and with hair as black as ebony, and because of that she was called Snow-White. And when the child was born, the queen died.

After a year the king took himself another wife. She was a beautiful woman, but she was proud and haughty and could not bear that anyone should be more beautiful than she. She had a wonderful mirror, and when she stood in front of it and looked in it and said:

> "Mirror, mirror on the wall,
> Who is fairest of us all?"

then the mirror would answer:

> "Queen, thou art the fairest of us all!"

Then she was satisfied, because she knew that the mirror spoke the truth.

But Snow-White kept growing, and kept growing more beautiful, and when she was seven years old, she was as beautiful as the bright day, and more beautiful than the Queen herself. Once when she asked her mirror:

> "Mirror, mirror on the wall,
> Who is fairest of us all?"

257

it answered:

> "Queen, thou art the fairest in this hall,
> But Snow-White's fairer than us all."

Then the Queen was horrified, and grew yellow and green with envy. From that hour on, whenever she saw Snow-White the heart in her body would turn over, she hated the girl so. And envy and pride, like weeds, kept growing higher and higher in her heart, so that day and night she had no peace. Then she called a huntsman and said: "Take the child out into the forest, I don't want to lay eyes on her again. You kill her, and bring me her lung and liver as a token."

The hunter obeyed, and took her out, and when he had drawn his hunting knife and was about to pierce Snow-White's innocent heart, she began to weep and said: "Oh, dear huntsman, spare my life! I'll run off into the wild forest and never come home again." And because she was so beautiful, the huntsman pitied her and said: "Run away then, you poor child."

"Soon the wild beasts will have eaten you," he thought, and yet it was as if a stone had been lifted from his heart not to have to kill her. And as a young boar just then came running by, he killed it, cut out its lung and liver, and brought them to the Queen as a token. The cook had to cook them in salt, and the wicked woman ate them up and thought that she had eaten Snow-White's lung and liver.

Now the poor child was all, all alone in the great forest, and so terrified that she stared at all the leaves on the trees and didn't know what to do. She began to run, and ran over the sharp stones and through the thorns, and the wild beasts sprang past her, but they did her no harm. She ran on till her feet wouldn't go any farther, and when it was almost evening she saw a little house and went inside to rest. Inside the house everything was small, but cleaner and neater than words will say. In the middle there stood a little table with a white tablecloth, and on it were seven little plates, each plate with its own spoon, and besides that, seven little knives and forks and seven little mugs. Against the wall were seven little beds, all in a row, spread with snow-white sheets. Because she was so hungry and thirsty, Snow-White ate a little of the vegetables and bread from each of the little plates, and drank a drop of wine from each little mug, since she didn't want to take all of anybody's. After that, because she was so tired, she lay down in a bed, but not a one would fit; this one was too long, the other was too short, and so on, until finally the seventh was just right, and she lay down in it, said her prayers, and went to sleep.

As soon as it had got all dark, the owners of the house came back. These were seven dwarfs who dug and delved for ore in the mountains. They lighted their seven little candles, and as soon as it got light in their little house, they saw that someone had been inside, because everything wasn't the way they'd left it.

The first said: "Who's been sitting in my little chair?"

The second said: "Who's been eating out of my little plate?"

The third said: "Who's been taking some of my bread?"

The fourth said: "Who's been eating my vegetables?"

The fifth said: "Who's been using my little fork?"

The sixth said: "Who's been cutting with my little knife?"

The seventh said: "Who's been drinking out of my little mug?"

Then the first looked around and saw that his bed was a little mussed, so he said: "Who's been lying on my little bed?" The others came running and cried out: "Someone's been lying in mine too." But the seventh, when he looked in his bed, saw Snow-White, who was lying in it fast asleep.

He called the others, who came running up and shouted in astonishment, holding up their little candles so that the light shone on Snow-White. "Oh my goodness gracious! Oh my goodness gracious!" cried they, "how beautiful the child is!" And they were so happy that they didn't wake her, but let her go on sleeping in the little bed. The seventh dwarf, though, slept with the others, an hour with each, till the night was over.

When it was morning Snow-White awoke, and when she saw the seven dwarfs she was frightened. They were friendly, though, and asked: "What's your name?"

"I'm named Snow-White," she answered.

"How did you get to our house?" went on the dwarfs. Then she told them that her stepmother had tried to have her killed, but that the huntsman had spared her life, and that she'd run the whole day and at last had found their house.

The dwarfs said: "If you'll look after our house for us, cook, make the beds, wash, sew, and knit, and if you'll keep everything clean and neat, then you can stay with us, and you shall lack for nothing."

"Yes," said Snow-White, "with all my heart," and stayed with them. She kept their house in order: in the morning the dwarfs went to the mountains and looked for gold and ores, in the evening they came back, and then their food had to be ready for them. In the daytime the little girl was alone, so the good dwarfs warned her and said: "Watch out for your stepmother. Soon she'll know you're here; be sure not to let anybody inside."

But the Queen, since she thought she had eaten Snow-White's lung and liver, was sure that she was the fairest of all. But one day she stood before her mirror and said:

> "Mirror, mirror on the wall,
> Who is fairest of us all?"

Then the mirror answered:

> "Queen, thou art the fairest that I see,
> But over the hills, where the seven dwarfs dwell,
> Snow-White is still alive and well,
> And there is none so fair as she."

This horrified her, because she knew that the mirror never told a lie; and she saw that the hunter had betrayed her, and that Snow-White was still alive. And she thought and thought about how to kill her, for as long as she wasn't the fairest in all the land, her envy gave her no rest. And when at last she thought of something, she painted her face and dressed herself like an old peddler woman, and nobody could have recognized her. In this disguise she went over the seven mountains to the seven dwarfs' house, knocked at the door, and called: "Lovely things for sale! Lovely things for sale!"

Snow-White looked out of the window and called: "Good day, dear lady, what have you to sell?"

"Good things, lovely things," she answered, "bodice laces of all colors," and she pulled out one that was woven of many-colored silk.

"It will be all right to let in the good old woman," thought Snow-White, unbolted the door, and bought herself some pretty laces.

"Child," said the old woman, "how it does become you! Come, I'll lace you up properly." Snow-White hadn't the least suspicion, and let the old woman lace her up with the new laces. But she laced so tight and laced so fast that it took Snow-White's breath away, and she fell down as if she were dead. "Now you're the most beautiful again," said the Queen to herself, and hurried away.

Not long after, at evening, the seven dwarfs came home, but how shocked they were to see their dear Snow-White lying on the ground; and she didn't move and she didn't stir, as if she were dead. They lifted her up, and when they saw how tightly she was laced, they cut the laces in two; then she began to breathe a little, and little by little returned to consciousness. When the dwarfs heard what had happened, they said: "The old peddler woman was no one else but that wicked Queen; be careful, don't ever let another soul inside when we're not with you."

But the wicked Queen, as soon as she'd got home, stood in front of the mirror and asked:

> "Mirror, mirror on the wall,
> Who is fairest of us all?"

It answered the same as ever:

> "Queen, thou art the fairest that I see,
> But over the hills, where the seven dwarfs dwell,
> Snow-White is still alive and well,
> And there is none so fair as she."

When she heard this all the blood rushed to her heart, she was so horrified, for she saw plainly that Snow-White was alive again. "But now," said she, "I'll think of something that really will put an end to you," and with the help of witchcraft, which she understood, she made a poisoned comb. Then she dressed herself up and took the shape of another old woman. So she went over the seven mountains to the seven dwarfs' house, knocked on the door, and called: "Lovely things for sale! Lovely things for sale!"

Snow-White looked out and said: "You may as well

go on, I'm not allowed to let anybody in."

"But surely you're allowed to look," said the old woman, and she took out the poisoned comb and held it up. It looked so nice to the child that she let herself be fooled, and opened the door. When they'd agreed on the price the old woman said: "Now, for once, I'll comb your hair properly." Poor Snow-White didn't suspect anything, and let the old woman do as she pleased. But hardly had she put the comb in Snow-White's hair than the poison in it began to work, and the girl fell down unconscious. "You paragon of beauty," cried the wicked woman, "now you're done for," and went away.

By good luck, though, it was almost evening, when the seven dwarfs came home. When they saw Snow-White lying on the ground as if she were dead, right away they suspected the stepmother and looked and found the poisoned comb. Hardly had they drawn it out than Snow-White returned to consciousness, and told them what had happened. Then they warned her all over again to stay in the house and open the door to no one.

At home the Queen stood in front of the mirror and said:

"Mirror, mirror on the wall,
Who is fairest of us all?"

It answered the same as ever:

"Queen, thou art the fairest that I see,
But over the hills, where the seven dwarfs dwell,
Snow-White is still alive and well,
And there is none so fair as she."

When she heard the mirror say that, she shook with rage. "Snow-White shall die," cried she, "even if it costs me my own life!" Then she went to a very secret, lonely room that no one ever came to, and there she made a poisoned apple. On the outside it was beautiful, white with red cheeks, so that anyone who saw it wanted it; but whoever ate even the least bite of it would die. When the apple was ready she painted her face and disguised herself as a farmer's wife, and then went over the seven mountains to the seven dwarfs' house. She knocked, and Snow-White put her head out of the window and said: "I'm not allowed to let anybody in, the seven dwarfs told me not to."

"That's all right with me," answered the farmer's wife. "I'll get rid of my apples without any trouble. Here, I'll give you one."

"No," said Snow-White, "I'm afraid to take it."

"Are you afraid of poison?" said the old woman. "Look, I'll cut the apple in two halves; you eat the red cheek and I'll eat the white." But the apple was so cunningly made that only the red part was poisoned. Snow-White longed for the lovely apple, and when she saw that the old woman was eating it, she couldn't resist it any longer, put out her hand, and took the poisoned half. But hardly had she a bite of it in her mouth than she fell down on the ground dead. Then the Queen gave her a dreadful look, laughed aloud, and cried: "White as snow, red as blood, black as ebony! This time the dwarfs can't wake you!"

And when, at home, she asked the mirror:

> "Mirror, mirror on the wall,
> Who is fairest of us all?"

at last it answered:

> "Queen, thou art the fairest of us all."

Then her envious heart had rest, as far as an envious heart can have rest.

When they came home at evening, the dwarfs found Snow-White lying on the ground. No breath came from her mouth, and she was dead. They lifted her up, looked to see if they could find anything poisonous, unlaced her, combed her hair, washed her with water and wine, but nothing helped; the dear child was dead and stayed dead. They laid her on a bier, and all seven of them sat down and wept for her, and wept for three whole days. Then they were going to bury her, but she still looked as fresh as though she were alive, and still had her beautiful red cheeks. They said: "We can't bury her in the black ground," and had made for her a coffin all of glass, into which one could see from every side, laid her in it, and wrote her name on it in golden letters, and that she was a king's daughter. Then they set the coffin out on the mountainside, and one of them always stayed by it and guarded it. And the animals, too, came and wept over Snow-White—first an owl, then a raven, and last of all a dove.

Now Snow-White lay in the coffin for a long, long

time, and her body didn't decay. She looked as if she were sleeping, for she was still as white as snow, as red as blood, and her hair was as black as ebony. But a king's son happened to come into the forest and went to the dwarfs' house to spend the night. He saw the coffin on the mountain, and the beautiful Snow-White inside, and read what was written on it in golden letters. Then he said to the dwarfs: "Let me have the coffin. I'll give you anything that you want for it."

But the dwarfs answered: "We wouldn't give it up for all the gold in the world."

Then he said: "Give it to me then, for I can't live without seeing Snow-White. I'll honor and prize her as my own beloved." When he spoke so, the good dwarfs took pity on him and gave him the coffin.

Now the king's son had his servants carry it away on their shoulders. They happened to stumble over a bush, and with the shock the poisoned piece of apple that Snow-White had bitten off came out of her throat. And in a little while she opened her eyes, lifted the lid of the coffin, sat up, and was alive again. "Oh, heavens, where am I?" cried she.

The king's son, full of joy, said: "You're with me," and told her what had happened, and said: "I love you more than anything in all the world. Come with me to my father's palace; you shall be my wife." And Snow-White loved him and went with him, and her wedding was celebrated with great pomp and splendor.

But Snow-White's wicked stepmother was invited to the feast. When she had put on her beautiful clothes, she stepped in front of the mirror and said:

> "Mirror, mirror on the wall,
> Who is fairest of us all?"

The mirror answered:

> "Queen, thou art the fairest in this hall,
> But the young queen's fairer than us all."

Then the wicked woman cursed and was so terrified and miserable, so completely miserable, that she didn't know what to do. At first she didn't want to go to the wedding at all, but it gave her no peace; she had to go and see the young queen. And as she went in she recognized Snow-White and, what with rage and terror, she stood there

273

and couldn't move. But they had already put iron slippers over a fire of coals, and they brought them in with tongs and set them before her. Then she had to put on the red-hot slippers and dance till she dropped down dead.

Rabbit's Bride

There was a woman and she had a daughter and they lived in a beautiful cabbage garden. In the wintertime there came a rabbit and ate all the cabbages, so the woman said to the daughter, "Go in the garden and chase the rabbit away." Says the girl to the rabbit, "Shoo shoo, rabbit, you're eating all our cabbage." Says the rabbit, "Come, girl, get up on my rabbit tail and come to my rabbit hut with me." But the girl doesn't want to. Next day the rabbit comes back and eats the cabbage, and the woman says to the daughter, "Go in the garden and chase the rabbit away." Says the girl to the rabbit, "Shoo shoo, rabbit, you're eating all our cabbage." Says the rabbit, "Come, girl, get up on my rabbit tail and come to my rabbit hut with me." The girl doesn't want to. On the third day the rabbit comes again and eats the cabbage, and the woman says to the daughter, "Go in the garden and chase the rabbit away." Says the girl, "Shoo shoo, rabbit, you're eating up our cabbage." Says the rabbit, "Come, girl, get up on my rabbit tail and come to my rabbit hut with me." The girl gets up on his rabbit tail and the rabbit carries her way away to his little hut and says, "Now cook me some green cabbage with millet and I'll go invite the wedding guests. And so the wedding guests assembled. (And who were the wedding guests? I can tell you that because I know all about it: All the rabbits were there, and the crow to act as parson to marry the bride and groom, and the fox was the sexton and the altar stood under the rainbow.) But the girl was sad, because she was lonely. Comes the rabbit and says, "Open the door, open the door, the wedding guests are ready for the party." The bride says nothing and cries. Rabbit goes away; rabbit comes back and says, "Open the door, open the door, the wedding guests are hungry." Again the bride says nothing and cries. Rabbit goes away. Rabbit comes back and says, "Open the door, open the door, the wedding guests are waiting." But the bride says nothing. Rabbit goes away but she makes a puppet out of straw and her clothes and gives it the wooden spoon to hold and sets it up in front of the kettle of millet and goes home to her mother. Rabbit comes back again and says, "Open the door, open the door," and opens the door and knocks the puppet on the head and the cap falls off.

And so rabbit sees that it is not his bride and goes away and is sad.

The Two Journeymen

Hill and valley never meet, but God's children do, sometimes even the good and the bad ones. And so it happened that a cobbler and a tailor who plied their trade from one town to the next met on the road. The tailor was a pretty little fellow, always jolly and in good spirits. He saw the cobbler walking toward him and could tell his trade by his knapsack, so he sang a song to tease him:

"Sew a stitch and pull a thread,

Paste it right and left with wax,
Hammer, hammer in the tacks."

The cobbler, who could not take a joke, made a face as if he'd swallowed vinegar and seemed about to take the little tailor by the scruff of the neck, but the little fellow began to laugh, offered him his bottle, and said, "I didn't mean it. Have a drink and wash down your bile." The shoemaker took a powerful swallow and the thundercloud began to pass from his face. He handed the bottle back to the tailor and said, "I've done it justice. They're always talking about drinking too much but never about the great thirst. Shall you and I go on our way together?" "It's fine with me," answered the tailor, "so long as you're heading for a big city where there's plenty of work." "Just what I had in mind," answered the cobbler. "There's no money to be made in the backwoods; country people would rather go barefoot." And so they went on together, setting one foot before the other like the weasel in the snow.

Time they had aplenty, these two, but little bread to break. When they came to a town they would make the rounds, calling on the men of their trade for work or handouts; and because the tailor looked so cheerful and pleasant and had such nice red cheeks, people liked giving to him, and if he was lucky the master's daughter let him have a kiss in the doorway to take along. When tailor and cobbler met again the tailor always had more in his knapsack than the bad-tempered cobbler, who would make a sour face and say, "The greater the scoundrel, the better his luck," but the tailor laughed, sang a song, and shared whatever he got with his friend. If his pocket tinkled with a couple of extra pennies, he'd call for the table to be laid and strike it in his delight, so that the glasses danced. His motto was "Easy come, easy go."

When they had been on the road for a while, they came to a great forest through which lay the way to the royal capital. But there were two paths and one took seven days, but the other took only two. Neither of the two journeymen knew which path was the shorter, so they sat down under an oak tree and talked over how they were to provide for themselves and how many days' bread they should carry with them. The cobbler said,

"One must think further than one travels. I will take bread for seven days." "Go on!" said the tailor, "haul seven days' bread on your back like a beast of burden so you can't even look about you! I trust in God and never worry. The money in my pocket is as good in summer as it is in winter, but bread dries out in hot weather and gets moldy besides; nor is my coat longer than I need to cover my ankles. Why shouldn't we hit upon the right path? Bread for two days, and that's that." And so each bought his bread and hoped for the best.

Inside the forest it was still as in a church. No wind stirred, no brook babbled, no bird sang. No ray of light could pass through the thickly leaved branches. The cobbler spoke never a word; the heavy bread pressed down on his back so that the sweat poured over his gloomy, ill-humored face. But the tailor was gay and skipped along, whistling on a leaf, singing his little song, and thought, "God in his heaven must be glad that I'm so happy!" And so it went for two days, but on the third day, when the forest would not come to an end and the tailor had finished all his bread, his heart did sink way down, but he never lost hope, trusted in God and his good luck. On the evening of the third day he lay down hungry under a tree and got up hungry next morning. And so it went on the fourth day, and when the cobbler took his seat on a fallen tree to partake of his meal, there was nothing for the tailor to do but look on. If he begged for a piece of bread, the other laughed and mocked him and said, "You were always so happy, for once you'll feel what it's like to be unhappy. It's the bird who sings too early in the morning that the hawk strikes down before the night." In short, he had no mercy. But on the fifth morning the poor tailor was unable to get up and could barely speak for weakness. His cheeks were white and his eyes were red and so the cobbler said, "I will give you a little piece of bread today, but in return I will cut your right eye out." The unhappy tailor, who longed to stay alive, had no choice. He wept one last time with his two eyes, and then held them up to the cobbler, who had a heart of stone and cut out the tailor's right eye with a sharp knife. The tailor remembered what his mother always used to say when she caught him nibbling in the larder: "Eat what you will, and suffer what you must." When he had

282

eaten his bit of bread so dearly bought, he got to his feet, forgot his misfortune, and comforted himself with the thought that he could still see well enough out of his other eye. But on the sixth day there was the hunger all over again and it nearly ate his heart out, and in the evening he fell down by a tree, and on the seventh day he could not get up for weakness, and death had him by the throat. And so the cobbler said, "I will be merciful once again and give you bread; but you must pay for it; I will cut out your other eye as well." And so the tailor understood the heedlessness of his life, begged the good Lord's forgiveness, and said, "Do what you will, I will suffer what I must. Only remember, Our Lord does not pass judgment each moment of the day, yet there shall come an hour when you will be punished for the evil you do me. I have not deserved it of you. In good times I shared with you whatever I had. My trade commands that one stitch chase another. If I have no eyes left I cannot sew and must go begging. Only do not leave me lying alone here after I am blind, or I shall perish." But the cobbler, who had driven God out of his heart, took the knife and cut out the tailor's other eye too. Then he gave him a piece of bread, handed him a stick, and led the tailor along behind him.

As the sun was setting they came out of the forest, and in a field near the edge of the forest stood a gallows and here the cobbler led the blind tailor and left him lying and went on his way. Out of weariness, pain, and hunger, the wretched man fell asleep and slept all night. When day dawned he woke but did not know where he was. On the gallows hung two poor sinners and on the head of each sat a crow, and one of the dead men began to speak: "Brother, are you awake?" "Yes, I am awake," answered the second. "Then I will tell you something," the first went on. "The dew which dripped down from the gallows over us last night could give the man who washes with it his eyesight back again. If the blind knew, there's many a one might have his eyes back who doesn't believe it possible." When the tailor heard this, he took out his handkerchief, pressed it to the grass, and when it was moist with dew he washed the sockets of his eyes with it. Immediately what the hanged man said came true: a pair of whole, healthy eyes filled his sockets. And the tailor saw the sun rising behind the

mountains. Before him, on the great plain, lay the imperial city with its splendid gates, and the hundred towers with golden buttons and crosses on their pinnacles began to glow. He could distinguish every leaf on the trees, saw the birds fly by and the gnats dancing in the air. He took a sewing needle from his pocket and threaded it as easily as ever, and his heart leaped for joy. He threw himself upon his knees, thanked God for the grace he had shown him, and said his morning blessing, nor did he forget to pray for the poor sinners hanging from the gallows like clappers in a bell, with the wind knocking one against the other. Then he took his bundle on his back, soon forgot the heartache he had suffered, and went singing and whistling on his way.

The first thing to cross his path was a brown foal cavorting in the open field. He grasped it by the mane, so as to swing himself up and ride into town, but the foal begged for its freedom. "I'm too young," it said. "Even a lightweight tailor like you would break my back, so let me go till I've grown strong. The time may come when I can make it up to you." "Run along," said the tailor. "I see that you're a flibbertigibbet just like me," and he spanked it over the rump with his switch so that it kicked its hind legs for joy, leaped over hedge and ditch, and chased off into the fields.

But the little tailor had eaten nothing since yesterday. "The sun fills my eyes," he said, "but where's the bread to fill my mouth? The first thing I run across that's anywhere near edible will have to be it." Just then, a stork came striding very gravely by. "Halt," cried the tailor, and grabbed it by the leg. "I don't know if you are edible or not, but my hunger doesn't leave me much choice. I'm going to cut off your head and roast you." "Don't do it," said the stork. "I am a sacred bird; nobody harms me, for I am very useful to mankind. Let me live, and I may repay you for it sometime or another." "Off you go, then, Cousin Longlegs," said the tailor. The stork rose into the air, letting his long legs dangle, and, without hurrying himself, flew away.

"This will never do," said the tailor to himself. "My hunger is getting worse and worse, and my stomach emptier and emptier. The next thing that crosses my path is lost." At that moment he saw a pair of ducks swimming on a pond. "You're just in time," he said, caught hold of one of them, and was about to wring its neck when the mother duck, who was hidden in the rushes, began to screech, making a great to-do, and came swimming up with her beak wide open, imploring him to have pity on her beloved children. "Only imagine," said she, "how your mother would carry on if someone did this to you." "Oh, all right," said the good-natured tailor, "you can keep your children," and set the captive back in the water. When he turned he was standing before a hollow tree and saw wild bees flying in and out. "Here's the reward for my good deed already," said the tailor. "This honey will revive me." But the queen bee came out and threatened him, saying, "If you touch my people and destroy my nest, our stingers shall pierce your skin like ten thousand fiery needles; but leave us in peace and go on your way and in return we will do you a service some day."

The little tailor saw there was nothing to be done here either. "Three empty platters," said he, "and nothing on the fourth is a poor sort of dinner." And so with his belly starving he dragged himself into the city, where the noon bell was pealing and the food at the inn was cooked and ready for him, and he sat down to dinner. When he had eaten his fill, he said, "And now I want some work," and walked around town looking for a master and soon found himself a good place, and because he had learned his trade from the ground up, it wasn't long before everyone wanted his new coat made by the little tailor. His fame grew day by day. "There's no way to improve my skill," said he, "yet every day I do better." And in the end the king appointed him Court Tailor.

But as it goes in this world, his former companion, the cobbler, had that same day been made Court Cobbler and when he caught sight of the tailor and saw that he had his two whole eyes again, his conscience tormented him. "Before he takes his revenge on me, I'll dig his grave for him," he thought. But he who digs another's grave falls in himself. In the evening, when he had closed up shop and dusk was falling, he sneaked off to the king and said, "Your majesty, that tailor is an impudent fellow. He has the gall to boast that he could find the crown lost in the olden days." "I'd like that," said the king, and the next morning he summoned the tailor and ordered him to produce the crown or leave town forever. "Oho," thought the tailor, "only a scoundrel gives more than he has. If this cantankerous king asks me to do what no man can, I won't wait till morning, I'll leave right now." And so he packed his bundle, but when he got outside the city gate he was sorry to leave his good fortune and face with his backside the town which had done so well by him.

He came to the pond where he had made the acquaintance of the ducks, and the old one, whose young he had spared, happened to be sitting on the shore preening herself with her beak. She knew him at once and asked why he hung his head. "You'll understand when you hear what happened to me," answered the tailor and told her his fate. "If that's all it is," said the duck, "there's no problem. The crown fell in the water and is lying on the bottom. We'll have it up in no time. You spread your handkerchief on the shore." The duck dove down with her twelve young ones and was back in five minutes, sitting in the middle of the crown, which rested on her feathers, and the twelve ducklings swam all around her, their beaks underneath the crown to help carry it. You can't imagine how it glittered in the sun like a hundred thousand brilliants. The tailor tied together the four corners of the cloth and brought the crown to the king, who was overjoyed and hung a golden chain around the tailor's neck.

When the cobbler saw that one trick had misfired, he thought up a second, presented himself before the king, and said, "Your majesty, that tailor is becoming impudent again. He has the gall to boast he could make a wax model of the whole palace with everything in it, freestanding or fixed, inside and out." The king summoned the tailor and ordered him to make a wax model of the whole palace and everything in it, free-standing or fixed, inside and out, and if he couldn't do it or left out so much as a nail in the wall, he would sit out the rest of his life in an underground prison. The tailor thought, "Worse and worse. No man can put up with this," threw his bundle across his shoulders, and marched off. When he came to the hollow tree, he sat down and hung his head. The bees flew out and the queen asked him if he had a stiff neck, the way he held his head.

"Oh no," answered the tailor, "it's a very different kind of trouble that makes me so sad," and told them what the king demanded of him. The bees began to buzz and hum among themselves and the queen bee said, "You just go back home, but tomorrow about this time come back, bring a nice big cloth, and everything will be all right." And so he went home, but the bees flew straight to the royal palace and through the open window, crept around in all the corners, and inspected every last thing. Then they flew back and copied everything in wax at such speed you would have thought you saw the palace growing before your eyes. It was all done by evening, and next morning, when the tailor came, there stood the whole splendid edifice, and not a nail in the wall, not a tile in the roof was missing, and it was delicate and snow-white and smelled sweet as honey besides. The tailor wrapped it carefully in his cloth and brought it to the king, who could not get over his surprise, set it up in the grandest of the halls, and in return made the tailor a present of a big stone house.

But the cobbler did not give up, appeared before the king a third time, and said, "Your majesty, the tailor has heard that no water will spring in the palace grounds and has the gall to boast that he could make it rise in the middle of your courtyard, man-high and clear as crystal." And so the king had the tailor brought in and said, "If by tomorrow there's no fountain springing man-high in my courtyard, as you have promised, the executioner shall, in that very spot, make you shorter by a head." The poor tailor did not stay to consider, but hurried out of the city gate, and because this time it was a matter of his very life, the tears rolled down his cheeks.

As he was walking full of grief, the foal whom he had given its freedom, and who had turned into a handsome, full-grown horse, came galloping along. "The time has come," it said, "when I can repay your good deed. I know what troubles you, but help is at hand. Just get up on my back. I could carry two your size." The tailor took heart again, mounted his back in one leap, and the horse ran to town at full gallop, straight into the royal courtyard, circled three times quick as lightning, and the third time crashed to the ground. In that same instant came a thunderous roar, a piece of earth flew like a cannon ball out of the middle of the courtyard, way into the air, over the palace, and in its wake rose a jet of water high as man and horse and clear as crystal, and caught the rays of the sun that danced upon it. When the king saw it, he stood up in amazement and came and embraced the little tailor in sight of all the people.

But his luck did not last. The king had daughters aplenty, one more beautiful than the next, but not a single son. And so the spiteful cobbler betook himself to the king a fourth time and said, "Your majesty, the tailor will not give up his impudent boasting. Now he has the gall to say that if he wished, he could have a son delivered to your majesty, by air." The king summoned the tailor and said, "If you have a son brought to me within nine days, you shall marry my eldest daughter." "The reward is certainly great," thought the little tailor, "and one would go out of one's way for it, but these are cherries that hang out of my reach. If I climb after them, the bough will break and I'll fall all the way down." He went home and sat down cross-legged on his worktable to consider what was to be done. "It'll never work," he finally cried. "There's no living in peace here." He tied his bundle and hurried out of the city gate. When he came to the meadow he caught sight of his old friend the stork, walking like some sage, up and down, stopping once in a while to make a close study of a frog he was about to swallow. The stork came to greet him. "I see," he began, "that you have your knapsack on your back. Why do you want to leave the city?" The tailor told him of the king's demand which he could not fulfill and bemoaned his ill fortune. "Don't grow any gray hairs over it," answered the stork. "I will help you in your need. I've been bringing the little babies to this city for a long while and there's no reason why I shouldn't fetch a little baby prince out of the well for once. You go home, don't fret. Nine days from today come to the court and I will be there too." The tailor went home and was at the palace in good time. It wasn't long before the stork came flying and knocked at the window. The tailor opened it and Cousin Longlegs stepped in cautiously and walked with measured tread over the smooth marble floors. In his beak he had a child, beautiful as an angel, who stretched his hands toward the queen. The stork put the baby in her lap and she hugged it and kissed it and was beside herself with joy. Before he flew away, the stork took his traveling bag from his shoulder and gave it to the queen. Inside were little paper cones full of colored candies to be shared among the little princesses. Only the eldest didn't get any. She got the happy tailor for a husband. "I feel," said the tailor, "as if I'd won first prize. My mother was right after all. She always said if a man trusts in God, and if he's lucky, he cannot fail."

The cobbler had to make the shoes in which the little tailor danced at his wedding and afterwards he was ordered to leave the town forever. The way to the forest led him past the gallows. Worn out with fury, anger, and the day's heat, he threw himself down, and as he closed his eyes to sleep, the two crows sitting on the hanged men's heads plummeted down with a loud screech and hacked out his two eyes. The cobbler in his madness ran into the forest, where he must have perished. Nobody has seen him since or heard anything about him.

Ferdinand Faithful
and Ferdinand Unfaithful

Once upon a time there was a man and a woman. As long as they were rich they didn't have any children, but when they became poor they got a little boy. They couldn't find him a godfather, so the man said he'd run over to the next village and see if he couldn't get one there. And as he was walking along he met a poor man who asked him where he was going. He said he was looking for a godfather for his little boy, because he was so poor nobody wanted to be godfather. "Oh," said the poor man, "you are poor and I am poor so I'll be the godfather, but I'm too poor to give the child anything. Go and tell the midwife to bring the child to the church." When everyone gets to the church, there's the beggar already inside and he gives the child the name of Ferdinand faithful.

Now as they were coming out, the beggar said, "You go along home. I can't give you anything so don't you give me anything either." But to the midwife he gave a key and told her to go home and give it to the father to keep until the child was fourteen years old, and then the boy should go up to the heath and there would be a castle with a keyhole which the key would fit and whatever was inside belonged to him. Now one day, when the child was seven years old and had grown a good deal, he went out to play with the other boys, and each one had got more from his godfather than the next. He was the only one who had nothing to tell and he cried and went home and said to his father, "Didn't I get anything at all from my godfather?" "Oh, yes," said the father. "What you got was a key. If there's a castle with a keyhole standing up on the heath, you just go over and unlock it." And so he went up on the heath but there was no castle to be heard or seen. Seven years later, when he is fourteen years old, he goes up again and there's the castle and he unlocks it and there's nothing in it except a horse, a white one, and the boy is so pleased with his horse he gets on its back and gallops home to his father. "Now I have a horse, I want to travel," says he.

Off he goes, and as he is riding along there's this writing quill lying on the road. First he is going to pick it up but then he thinks to himself, You could really let it lie where it is, you are sure to find a quill wherever you're going, if you happen to need one, and as he is riding away, he hears something calling behind him, "Ferdinand faithful, take it with you." He looks around, doesn't see anybody, goes back, and picks it up. When he has ridden for a while he comes to a river and there is a fish lying on the shore flapping and snapping for air, and so he says, "Wait a moment, my dear fish, and I'll help you get back into the water," takes it by the tail, and throws it into the river, and the fish sticks its head out of the water and says, "Because you helped me out of the mud, I'll give you a flute to pipe on. If you're ever in need, pipe, and I will come and help you, or if you should ever drop anything into the water, you just pipe and I will hand it up to you." And so he rides on and there comes this man walking along and asks him where he is going. "Oh, to the next place." And what's his name? "Ferdinand faithful." "Look at that, then we have almost the same name! I am called Ferdinand unfaithful." So they continue on their way together as far as the next village and go into the inn.

Now the trouble was that this Ferdinand unfaithful knew everything the other person was thinking or planning. He knew these things by means of all kinds of evil arts. Now in this inn there was a stouthearted girl with a nice open face who carried herself so nicely and she fell in love with Ferdinand faithful because he was a nice-looking boy and she asked him where he was going. Oh, traveling around. And so she said why didn't he stay here, there was a king in the country and he was sure to want a servant or an outrider and why not go into his service. He answered that he couldn't very well go to someone and offer himself, but the girl said, "Well, then I'll do it for you." And so she went right to the king and told him she knew a nice-looking servant for him. That was fine by the king and he had him summoned and would have made him his servant, but Ferdinand faithful liked being an outrider better because wherever his horse was, that's where he wanted to be, and so the king made him an outrider. When Ferdinand unfaithful found out about this he said to the girl, "Wait a minute, are you going to help him and not me?" "Oh," said the girl, "I'll help you too." She thought, You'd better stay friends with this one because you can't trust him, so she goes to the king and offers him as a servant and that's fine with the king.

Now mornings, when Ferdinand unfaithful was dressing his master, the king was always complaining and carrying on: "Oh, if I only had my beloved here with me." Ferdinand unfaithful was always looking to make trouble for Ferdinand faithful and one day, when the king was complaining again, he said, "You have your outrider. Why don't you send him to go and get her for you and if he doesn't, let his head be laid at his feet." And so the king has Ferdinand faithful summoned and tells him he has a beloved there and there and to go get her, and if he doesn't, he shall die.

Ferdinand faithful went to his white horse in the stable and cried and complained. "Oh, what an unhappy creature am I," but he hears somebody calling behind him: "Ferdinand faithful, what are you crying for?" He looks around, doesn't see anybody, and goes on lamenting and complaining: "Oh, my dear horse, I have to leave you now and I'm going to die." And again there is this voice calling, "Ferdinand faithful, what are you crying for?" and only now does he see that it is his little white horse that is asking the question. "Is that you, dear horse? And can you talk?" and he goes on, "I am supposed to go there and there to fetch the bride. You wouldn't know how I am to go about it, would you?" and so the white horse answers, "You just go to the king and tell him to give you what you need and you will go and fetch the bride. If he gives you a ship full of meat and a ship full of bread, you'll manage everything because there are great big giants on the water and if you didn't bring them any meat they would tear you apart, and there are great big birds who would pick the eyes out of your head if you didn't bring any bread for them." And so the king ordered all the butchers in the land to butcher and all the bakers to bake so as to fill the ships. And when they are filled up, the little white horse says to Ferdinand faithful, "Now get on my back and ride me onto the boat and when the giants come say:

> "Hush up, my little giants.
> I've not forgotten you
> And brought you something too.

and when the birds come, then you say again:

> "Hush up, dear little birdies.
> I've not forgotten you
> And brought you something too.

Then they won't do you any harm and when you get to the castle the giants will help you. Go into the castle and take a couple of giants with you and the princess will be lying there, asleep, but you mustn't wake her. Just have the giants pick her up, bed and all, and carry

her into the ship." And everything happened just as
the horse had said and Ferdinand faithful gave the
giants and the birds what he had brought for them and
in return the giants helped carry the princess in her
bed. But when she comes to the king she says she cannot live, she has to have her papers that were left behind in the castle. And so Ferdinand faithful, at the
instigation of Ferdinand unfaithful, is summoned and
the king orders him to go fetch the papers from the
castle or die. And so he goes back to the stable and
cries and says, "Dear horse, now I have to leave you
again. Whatever are we going to do?" And so the white
horse says he should load up the ships again. (And so
it goes just like the last time and the giants and the
birds are fed and appeased with the meat.) When they
get to the castle the white horse says he should walk
into the princess's bedroom, the papers are on the desk.
And so Ferdinand faithful goes in and fetches them.
And when they are on the high seas he drops his writing quill in the water and the horse says, "Now I can't
help you," and he remembers the flute and starts piping
and the fish comes and has the quill in his mouth and

307

reaches it up to him. Then he brings the papers to the castle and the wedding is celebrated.

However, the queen did not like the king very much because he did not have a nose; she liked Ferdinand faithful. So one day, when all the gentlemen of the court were assembled, the queen said that she knew a good trick: she could chop off someone's head and put it back again and someone should come and try it. Nobody wanted to be first, and so Ferdinand faithful, again at the instigation of Ferdinand unfaithful, had to be the one, and she chopped off his head and put it back on again and it healed right away so that he looked as if he had a red thread around his neck. And so the king said, "My child, where did you learn that?" "Oh, well," said she, "it's a talent I have. Shall I try it on you?" "Oh, yes," says he, and she chops off his head but doesn't put it back and acts as if she can't get it on again. It just will not and will not stay put. And so the king is buried and she marries Ferdinand faithful.

But Ferdinand faithful is always riding his white horse. One day when he is sitting on its back, it tells him to ride to a new pasture, it'll let him know which one, and to gallop three times around it, and when he has done this the white horse stands up on its hind legs and turns into a prince.

Mrs. Gertrude

Once upon a time there was a little girl and she was obstinate and willful and did not obey her parents when they spoke to her. What good can come to such a child? One day she said to her parents, "I've heard so much talk about Mrs. Gertrude I want to go and see her. People say her house is very strange and they say there are such queer goings on there that I've become curious." Her parents strictly forbade her and said, "Mrs. Gertrude is an evil woman who does wicked things. If you go there, you are no longer our child." But the girl

paid no attention, and though her parents had told her no, went anyway, and when she got to Mrs. Gertrude, Mrs. Gertrude said, "Why are you so pale?" "Ah," the girl answered, trembling all over, "because I'm frightened at the things I've seen." "What have you seen?" "I saw a black man on your stairs." "That was a collier." "Then I saw a green man." "That was a hunter." "And then I saw a man red as blood." "That was a butcher." "Ah, but, Mrs. Gertrude, it made my skin crawl when I looked through the window and didn't see you but it must have been the devil himself with his head on fire." "Oho," said she, "so you have seen the witch in her true ornament. I have been expecting you a long time and have hankered for you, you're going to brighten up my house for me." And she changed the little girl into a log and threw it into the fire. And when it was at full glow she sat down beside it, warmed herself, and said, "There now, isn't that nice and bright!"

The Juniper Tree

It is a long time ago now, as much as two thousand years maybe, that there was a rich man and he had a wife and she was beautiful and good, and they loved each other very much but they had no children even though they wanted some so much, the wife prayed and prayed for one both day and night, and still they did not and they did not get one. In front of their house was a yard and in the yard stood a juniper tree. Once, in wintertime, the woman stood under the tree and peeled herself an apple, and as she was peeling the apple she cut her finger and the blood fell onto the snow. "Ah," said the woman and sighed a deep sigh, and she looked at the blood before her and her heart ached. "If I only had a child as red as blood and as white as snow." And as she said it, it made her feel very happy, as if it was really going to happen. And so she went into the house, and a month went by, the snow was gone; and two months, and everything was green; and three months, and the flowers came up out of the ground; and four months, and all the trees in the woods sprouted and the green branches grew dense and tangled with one another and the little birds sang so that the woods echoed, and the blossoms fell from the trees; and so five months were gone, and she stood under the juniper tree and it smelled so sweet her heart leaped and she fell on her knees and was beside herself with happiness; and when six months had gone by, the fruit grew round and heavy and she was very still; and seven months, and she snatched the juniper berries and ate them so greedily she became sad and ill; and so the eighth month went by, and she called her husband and cried and said, "When I die, bury me under the juniper." And she was comforted and felt happy, but when the nine months were gone, she had a child as white as snow and as red as blood and when she saw it she was so happy that she died.

And so her husband buried her under the juniper tree and began to cry and cried very bitterly; and then for a time he cried more gently and when he had cried some more he stopped crying and more time passed and he took himself another wife.

By the second wife he had a daughter, but the child of his first wife was a little son as red as blood and as white as snow. Now when the woman looked at her daughter she loved her so, but looking at the little boy cut her to the heart. It seemed that wherever he was standing, he was always in her way and then she kept wondering how to get the whole fortune just for her daughter, and the evil one got into her so that she began to hate the little boy and would push him around from one corner to the other and punch him here and pinch him there so that the poor child was always in a fright. When he came home from school there was no quiet place where he could be.

Once the woman had gone upstairs and her little daughter came up too and said, "Mother, can I have an apple?" "Yes, my child," said the woman and gave her a beautiful apple out of the chest. Now this chest had a great heavy lid with a sharp iron lock. "Mother," said the little daughter, "couldn't brother have one too?" This upset the woman but she said, "He can have one when he gets back from school." And as she looked out of the window she saw him coming and it was just as if the devil got into her and she reached out and snatched the apple out of her daughter's hand and said, "You can't have one till your brother comes," and threw the apple back into the chest and closed the lid. And then the little boy came in the door and the evil one made her speak kindly to him and she said, "My son, would you like an apple?" and looked at him full of hatred. "Mother," said the little boy, "how strange and wild you look! Please give me an apple." And it was as if she must still draw him on and she said, "Come with me," and lifted up the lid. "You can pick out your own apple." And as the little boy leaned in, the evil one spoke in her ear. Crunch! she slammed the lid shut so

317

that the head flew off and rolled among the red apples. And now terror overwhelmed her and she thought, "How can I get myself out of this?" and so she went up to her room, to her wardrobe, and out of the top drawer she took a white cloth and set the head back on the neck and tied the scarf around it in such a way that you couldn't see anything and set him on a chair in front of the door and put the apple in his hand.

And little Ann Marie came into the kitchen where her mother was standing by the fire with a pot of hot water in front of her that she kept stirring around and around. "Mother," said Ann Marie, "brother is sitting in front of the door. He looks so white and has an apple in his hand. I asked him to give me the apple but he wouldn't answer me, and it made my flesh creep!" "Go back out," said her mother, "and if he won't answer you, you box his ears for him." And so Ann Marie went out and said, "Brother, give me your apple," but he said nothing and so she boxed his ears, and his head fell off and she was horror-stricken and began to cry and to scream and ran to her mother and said, "Oh, Mother, I've hit my brother and knocked his head off,"

318

and cried and cried and could not stop. "Ann Marie," said the mother, "what have you done! But you just keep quiet and nobody will know. After all, it can't be helped now; we will stew him in a sour broth." And so the mother took the little boy and hacked him in pieces and put the pieces in the pot and stewed him in the sour broth. But Ann Marie stood by and cried and cried and the tears fell in the pot so that it didn't need any salt.

When the father came home he sat down to supper and said, "And where is my son?" And so the mother brought a big dish of black stew and Ann Marie cried and couldn't stop crying. And again the father said, "Where is my son?" "Oh," said the mother, "he's gone on a trip. He went to his mother's great-uncle and wants to stay there for a while." "What's he going to do there? And never even said goodbye to me!" "Oh, he wanted so much to go, he asked me if he could stay six weeks; they'll take good care of him there." "Ah," said the man, "why am I feeling so sad? It doesn't seem right, somehow. He might at least have come and said goodbye to me!" With that he began to eat and said,

"Ann Marie, what are you crying for? You'll see, your brother will be back." Then he said, "Ah, wife, what good food this is! Give me some more." And the more he ate the more he wanted, and said, "Give me more. You can't have any of it; it's as if all of this were for me." And he ate and ate, and threw the bones under the table, and finished it all up. But Ann Marie went to her chest of drawers and took her best silk scarf out of the bottom drawer and fetched every last little bone from under the table and tied them up in the silk cloth and carried them outside, weeping tears of blood. Then she laid them under the juniper tree in the green grass and as soon as she had laid them there she felt so much better and didn't cry any more. But the juniper began to stir and the branches kept opening out and coming back together again, just like someone who is really happy and goes like this with his hands. And then there was a sort of mist coming out of the tree and right in this mist it burned like fire and out of the fire flew this lovely bird that sang oh, so gloriously sweet and flew high into the air and when it was gone the juniper tree was just the way it had always been and

the cloth with the bones was gone. But Ann Marie felt so light of heart and so gay, just as if her brother were still alive. And so she went back into the house and was happy and sat down at the table and ate.

But the bird flew away and sat down on the roof of the goldsmith's house and began to sing:

> "My mother she butchered me,
> My father he ate me,
> My sister, little Ann Marie,
> She gathered up the bones of me
> And tied them in a silken cloth
> To lay under the juniper.
> Tweet twee, what a pretty bird am I!"

The goldsmith was sitting in his workshop, making a golden chain, and he heard the bird that sat on his roof and sang, and it seemed so beautiful to him. He got up and as he was walking across the doorstep he lost one of his slippers. But he kept walking right out into the middle of the street with one slipper and one stocking foot; he had his apron tied around his middle and in one hand he had the golden chain and in the other

the pliers and the sun shone so brightly into the street.
And he just stood there and looked at the bird. "Bird,"
said he, "how beautifully you sing! Sing that piece
again." "No," said the bird, "the second time I don't
sing for nothing. Give me the golden chain and I'll sing
it again." "Here," said the goldsmith, "take the golden
chain, now sing it again." And so the bird came and
took the golden chain in its right claw and sat in front
of the goldsmith and sang:

> "My mother she butchered me,
>   My father he ate me,
>   My sister, little Ann Marie,
>   She gathered up the bones of me
>   And tied them in a silken cloth
>   To lay under the juniper.
>   Tweet twee, what a pretty bird am I!"

And so the bird flew off to a cobbler's and sat down on
the roof and sang:

> "My mother she butchered me,
>   My father he ate me,

The Juniper Tree

My sister, little Ann Marie,
She gathered up the bones of me
And tied them in a silken cloth
To lay under the juniper.
Tweet twee, what a pretty bird am I!"

The cobbler heard it and ran out of the door in his shirtsleeves and looked up to the roof and had to hold his hand over his eyes so the sun would not blind him. "Bird," said he, "how beautifully you sing!" And he called in through the door, "Wife, come out here a moment. There's a bird here, look at this bird! And how it can sing!" And he called his daughter and the children and the servants, the apprentice and the maid, and they all came into the street and saw the bird, how pretty it was, and it had such red feathers and green feathers and round the neck it was like pure gold and its eyes glittered in its head like stars. "Bird," said the cobbler, "sing me that piece again." "No," said the bird, "the second time I don't sing for nothing. You have to give me a present." "Wife," said the man, "go to the attic; up on the top shelf is a pair of red shoes, bring them

325

down." And so the wife went up and got the shoes. "Here, bird," said the man, "now sing that piece again." And so the bird came and took the shoes in its left claw and flew back up to the roof and sang:

> "My mother she butchered me,
>   My father he ate me,
>   My sister, little Ann Marie,
>   She gathered up the bones of me
>   And tied them in a silken cloth
>   To lay under the juniper.
>   Tweet twee, what a pretty bird am I!"

And when it had finished singing, it flew away; it held the chain in its right claw and the shoes in its left, and flew far away to a mill and the mill went, "Clickety-clack, clickety-clack, clickety-clack." And in the door of the mill sat twenty of the miller's men hewing a new millstone and they chopped, "Chip-chop, chip-chop, chip-chop," and the mill went, "Clickety-clack, clickety-clack, clickety-clack." And so the bird went and sat on the linden tree that stood in front of the mill, and sang:

The Juniper Tree

"My mother she butchered me,"

and one of them stopped,

"My father he ate me,"

and two more stopped to listen,

"My sister, little Ann Marie,"

and four more stopped,

"She gathered up the bones of me
And tied them in a silken cloth,"

now there were only eight still chopping,

"To lay,"

now only five,

"under the juniper,"

now only one,

"Tweet twee, what a pretty bird am I!"

And so the last one stopped too and he had heard only
the last part. "Bird," said he, "how beautifully you sing!

I want to hear it too. Sing it again." "No," said the bird, "the second time I don't sing for nothing. Give me the millstone and I'll sing it again." "Yes," said he, "if it belonged to me alone, you could have it." "Yes," the others said, "if he sings again he can have it." And so the bird came down and the millers, all twenty of them, set the beam to and raised up the stone, "Heave-ho-hup, heave-ho-hup, heave-ho-hup." And the bird stuck its neck through the hole and put it on as if it were a collar and flew back into the tree and sang:

> "My mother she butchered me,
>   My father he ate me,
>   My sister, little Ann Marie,
>   She gathered up the bones of me
>   And tied them in a silken cloth
>   To lay under the juniper.
>   Tweet twee, what a pretty bird am I!"

And when it had finished singing, it spread its wings, and in the right claw it carried the chain, and the shoes in the left, and around the neck it wore the millstone, and flew all the way back to its father's house.

The Juniper Tree

Inside, the father, the mother, and Ann Marie were sitting at the table and the father said, "Ah, suddenly my heart feels so easy. Why do I feel so wonderfully good?" "No," said the mother, "I'm just so frightened, as if there was a great storm coming." But Ann Marie sat and cried and cried and right then the bird came flying along and as it sat down on the roof the father said, "How happy I'm feeling! And outside the sun is shining so brightly! It's just as if I were going to meet an old friend." "No," said the wife, "I'm so frightened! My teeth are chattering and it's as if I had fire in my veins." And she tore at her bodice to loosen it, but Ann Marie sat in a corner crying and held her plate in front of her eyes and cried so hard she was getting it wet and messy. And so the bird sat in the juniper tree and sang:

"My mother she butchered me"

And so then the mother stopped her ears up and squeezed her eyes shut and did not want to see or hear, but in her ears it roared like the wildest of storms and her eyes burned and twitched like lightning.

"My father he ate me"

"Ah, mother," said the man, "what a pretty bird and how sweetly it sings, and the sun so warm, and everything smells like cinnamon."

"My sister, little Ann Marie"

And Ann Marie laid her head on her knees and just kept crying and crying, but the man said, "I'm going outside, I must see the bird close up." "Don't go!" said the woman. "I feel as if the whole house were trembling and in flames." But the man went outside and looked at the bird:

> "She gathered up the bones of me
>   And tied them in a silken cloth
>   To lay under the juniper.
>   Tweet twee, what a pretty bird am I!"

With this the bird let the golden chain fall, and it fell right around the man's neck and looked so well on him, and he went inside and he said, "Look at the pretty bird, what a pretty golden chain it gave me for a present, and how pretty it is to look at!" But the woman was so frightened she fell full length on the floor and the cap fell off her head. And still the bird sang.

"My mother she butchered me"

"I wish I were a thousand miles under the earth so that I wouldn't have to hear it."

"My father he ate me"

And the woman lay there as if she were dead.

"My sister, little Ann Marie"

"Ah," said Ann Marie, "I'm going out too to see if the bird has a present for me," and so she went out.

"She gathered up the bones of me
And tied them in a silken cloth,"

and here it threw the shoes down to her.

"To lay under the juniper.
Tweet twee, what a pretty bird am I!"

And she felt so lighthearted and gay. She put on the new red shoes and came dancing and skipping into the house. "Ah," said she, "I was so sad when I went outside, and now I feel so much better. What a wonderful bird it is! It gave me a pair of red shoes for a present." "No," said the woman and she jumped up and her hair stood straight on end like flaming fire. "It's as if the world were coming to an end. I'm going out and maybe I will feel better too." And as she came out of the door, crunch! the bird threw the millstone on her head and she was squashed. The father and Ann Marie heard it and came out. There was steam and flames and fire rising from the spot, and when they were gone, there stood the little brother and he took his father and Ann Marie by the hand and the three of them were so happy and went into the house and sat down at the table and ate their supper.

Printed and bound by Arcata Graphics / Halliday
Designed by Atha Tehon and Maurice Sendak